WHAT

IT

TAKES

I0630301

WHAT
IT
TAKES

A
novella
by

JOSEPH
TORRA

Quale Press

On the cover: digital photograph by Carlo Lombardo

ISBN: 978–1–935835–22–6 trade paperback edition

LCCN: 2018935434

Quale Press
www.quale.com

WHAT
IT
TAKES

//////

I untangle several dust-covered extension cords—the first a cheap one cracked through to the wires, the second sturdier and longer, and the third a twenty-five-foot outdoor cord that hasn't been used since the last time Laura strung Christmas lights. Shelves are caked with dust and mouse shit, so I suck it all up with the indoor/outdoor vacuum, then I replace the can of Raid, several half-full cans of paint, an old-fashioned squirt oilcan, sandpaper, a drill, several containers of drill bits, a can of varnish, unopened boxes of mice poison, adhesive remover, wood finish, window cleaner, wood filler and caulking guns. I've never used any of this stuff. This is Laura's domain. Six months ago to the day, Laura died. Today I turn sixty-two. Yesterday I bought a Black+Decker Weed-Whacker at Home Depot. Laura knew every corner of that place. I never stepped foot until this summer. They have everything I might need for the house. She worked part-time, took care of the kids, cooked, cleaned, fixed minor electrical problems, painted, papered and anything else that needed to be done. The yard simply went to hell until she took to gardening. If Laura wanted Freddy to cut the grass, Freddy wouldn't. Laura said the reason Freddy wouldn't cut the grass is because I wouldn't cut the grass. Later, Laura reinvented the yard—the patio her crowning achievement. In the far corner of the basement sit Freddy's weights and bench beside which Jan's saddle rests on its stand. A pair of white figure skates, probably from Jan's middle school years, hangs from the ceiling. I might hear from them today, it being my birthday— though I never considered birthdays anything special. After the diagnosis, Laura read up on health and nutrition and began eating a plant-based diet. I stuck with my frozen dinners and potato chips. Near the end, Laura went back to eating whatever she wanted. She'd lost her taste for food, content with a piece of cake and a glass of milk. I tried to be there for her. My early retirement had been a blessing. At least we had time together. Sometimes near the very end, I wished it would be over. Even she wanted to go. I'm ready to go she said. Laura survived nearly four years after the news. That kind of cancer ran in her family—same thing that got her aunt and two cousins. During that time I found myself fantasizing about what I would do after she died. Sell the house and buy a condominium, or rent an apartment and have all the money from the house. I learned from my father about paying double mortgage payments. The one good thing I got from him, and house had been paid off for years. I moved into the guest room after the kids left home—hibernating, watching television and eating snacks. Later, when I got a computer, I'd go online. Nothing specific, wherever I landed—human-interest stories, local, national or international news but I mostly read headlines. I hated my job. I don't have any friends. I've never been passionate about anything—at a certain point in my life I got forced into something. After community college I wanted to go on to the state college. My father worked for the state his entire life, the highway department. In the winter he plowed and salted and in the summer repaired roads where they fixed the damage done during winter. James Chance had English, Scotch, German and I don't know what else in his blood. My mother Elsie part French-Canadian, part Native American, part Irish and part Austrian. My father played the social game when his needs could be served. Through some connection and a few favors, he secured me an entry-level administrative position in the state's human resources division. He told me take the job and I wouldn't have to do another day's work the rest of my life. I took the job and never made it to the state college. Forty years later, the economy forced me out with an early retirement. I felt lucky, even though the money was less than if I made it to sixty-five. Each morning I dreaded the sound of that alarm and when I woke I fought back a sickness thinking about another eight hours. I'd calculate the last time I called in and think could I do it again this soon? Now my bills are minimal. The monthly social security and state pension will carry me until I die, which at my age could be tonight in bed. Who'll find me? When? What if I get ten more years? Twenty? Will there be enough tasks to keep me busy? Why Laura and not me?

//////

I took a shower and missed Jan's birthday call. Her message says happy birthday Dad, thinking of you. Freddy didn't phone. Last time we talked he was working at a restaurant in Rhode Island. I did more stretches than usual this morning and feel limber. Instead of turning around downtown I keep on walking. Last night for my birthday I treated myself to a piece of vegan carrot cake. I bought it at the new café downtown. The woman who owns the place bakes it herself. She bakes good bread too. It's a hangout for young people. But they're friendly enough. I could cut back into town for a snack at the café but instead I strike out for the river road. Back home I cook steel-cut oatmeal with raisins and crushed walnuts washed down with a cup of green tea. Paging through one of Laura's magazines, I land on an article about enzymes and amino acids. I can't make sense of it and skip ahead to a story with a penciled note in the margin. It's my name, underlined. Laura often made notes or highlighted passages in her books and magazines. But she'd never referred to me. It's about how people who feel depressed and isolated are more likely to die prematurely. How socializing is part of the evolutionary process. She loved socializing. If not with her two sisters, there were girlfriends from high school with whom she kept in touch. In the early days I tried to do the visits—Sunday cookouts with her family, dinners with her friend Lucinda and her husband. And there were traditions like switching Thanksgiving from house to house each year. I hated how Laura's siblings went through their routine where someone would forget whose turn it was to host—Jenny you didn't do it last year last year Laura hosted, you did it the year before that. Oh, Jenny would say, it's all a blur to me. They knew whose turn, it was all just for some kind of show. In time Laura attended most events alone. Nothing derailed me more than having to entertain. Eventually, Laura stopped inviting friends to the house. After my father died, I occasionally visited my mother. I'd stay an hour or so—always an excuse why I had to go. Junior lives two towns over in Haywood. When Laura died and he came to the funeral it was the first time I'd seen him in fifteen years. I flip ahead to pictures of silken tofu chocolate, chilled soba noodles, whole wheat penne with roasted vegetables, multi-grain griddlecakes. The griddlecakes I remember from the time Laura made them on Thanksgiving morning—when Freddy moved home while she was having chemotherapy. I opted for my Pop Tarts. Other than a foray into the occasional bacon and two eggs sunny, my breakfast of choice was two cups of coffee, cream with two sugars, and Pop Tarts, preferably frosted. No Pop Tarts, donuts would do. Lunch could be anything, and I had all morning to think about it. Most of the people in the office sent out for lunch. I preferred to go out, alone. Sometimes I opted for pizza, other times fast food, and on Fridays Chinese at the nearby Golden Dragon. The number seven luncheon special: chicken fingers, spare ribs, fried rice and a cup of hot and sour soup. This morning I stack all the weights in an orderly pile to take a tally. There are more than I thought. The bench appears to be in good condition. I place my hand flat on the seat of Jan's saddle—her twelfth birthday present. She'd been riding since ten. When I recently asked her she said she didn't want the saddle and I could do what I wanted with it. I shovel the last of the debris off the basement floor and toss it into the trash barrel. It's been a good week's work. The entire basement cleaned and organized. I've thrown out so much trash over the past months I had to buy more trash barrels at Home Depot. Laura bought Jan a good saddle. It's worth a few bucks but I'll price it low. Some kid will have a lot of fun with it. The weights I'll price even lower because it will be hard to haul them away. An email came in about the bike. Laura bought it when she first got the news. She spent a lot of money too, and rode weather permitting until she no longer could. Using Craigslist I've sold Laura's car, one of the televisions, a camera and a computer. The weights, saddle and bike are the last of it. The storage room in the basement was the biggest mess to deal with—old suitcases, mildew-laden sleeping bags, a tent worn through at the seams, boxes of assorted gadgets, bags that contained shoes or clothing. An old electric train set looked new—a Christmas or birthday present for Freddy? The basement took some water in the big storm of '07—and again not long before Laura died. I was afraid of mold in the storage room. The carpet never fully dried. I tore the carpet out and discovered a rotting pine floor underneath and took my hammer and crowbar to the floor. In places with more water damage, the floor came up easy. But the dry boards were harder and I worked up a sweat. I loaded the broken floor pieces into trash barrels. We only got trash collection fifteen years ago. Up until then, everything went to the dump. Every Saturday morning I filled the trunk and drove to the crowded dump. When we bought the house there were still a few farms around. Ours was the last house at the end of a dead end on Meadow Road. From our house, woodlots extended out to Route 115. Now everything's developed. Year after year, I drove back and forth to work there were new roads and developments. I decided to put an indoor-outdoor carpet in the storage room. That's what they recommend online. Tomorrow I'll make a Home Depot run.

/////

The young woman buys Laura's bike without riding it.
She sits on it to check the size. A perfect fit. I tell her I
would have kept it myself but it's too small. The price is
right and she knows it. Is she from around here? She
says East Haywood on Taylor's Hill. I hunted on Taylor's
Hill as a boy. Am I a hunter she asks with a tone of
judgment. Not for years. Back then everybody hunted.
There weren't any houses on Taylor's Hill—all woods,
before they developed it. She loads the bike into her
van. I figure she's not long out of college and consider
telling her that the bike belonged to my wife who died of
cancer. But I don't get the chance. She drives away and
when I wave she gives me a lukewarm smile. We'd enter
the woods before daylight, using flashlights. I never
liked being in the woods in the dark. There were many
deer on Taylor's Hill and on opening day the locals
descended upon it. My father, younger brother Ronnie
Chance, or "Fat" Chance as some called him, and my
oldest brother Jimmy, or Junior, would be out before

anyone, and take our stands at strategic locations. Other hunters arrived and entered the woods and they'd spook the deer up the hill past my father or one of us and we'd be the first that season to bag a deer. Slow to find my way in the woods, I feared getting lost and carried two compasses. One time hunting on the other side of Taylor's Hill where the forest stretched out uninterrupted all the way to New Hampshire—I took a compass reading and to my surprise, the direction I assumed south read north. So certain that I knew the right direction I ignored the compass and walked lost for several hours working myself into a state of hysterics. Junior found me wandering in circles. Always trust your compass Junior told me. From then on I never entered the woods without two compasses and whenever I doubted the first reading I checked the second compass and they never disagreed. Junior nicknamed me Chief Two-Compasses. One hunting morning I had to answer nature's call, leaned my gun against a tree and did my business. I heard something approaching from the distance, steps on crunchy November leaves, and tried to hurry things as the noise came directly towards me. At first, I thought it might be another hunter but then the idea struck that it could be a deer and I quickly pulled up my pants reached for my gun and a six-point buck stepped out from behind a stand of pines and stared. I raised the shotgun, clicked the safety, and squeezed the slug barrel trigger without sighting the deer. At the explosion, the deer bounded up the hill its white tail flag high in the air. Near the crest of the hill and still within range, the animal stopped and turned broadside looking directly at me and I took aim and fired the buckshot barrel of the twelve-gauge double. The deer turned unmarked and hopped over the top of the hill. My father was angry and reprimanded me. We had the chance to be the first to take a deer, and a good deer, and I missed one standing right in front of me. He suggested next time he'd take my sister. But I had no sister. The following year I missed a doe on opening morning. Fortunately, Ronnie and Junior each shot a deer that day so nothing much was made of it. A year later I shot my first deer. An average-sized doe walked within forty feet and looked me in the eye and I raised the gun and fired the buckshot barrel so as not to take any chances. Her legs gave out and she dropped to the ground. I ran to the animal, she tried to stand and seemed to be looking at me so I placed the shotgun barrel behind her ear and finished her off with the slug. I dreamed about that deer. I still do. How she looked at me with such panic and I put the gun behind her ear and pulled the trigger. When deer season came the following year I told my father and brothers I didn't want to go hunting. They took it personally. It was a family thing. The next year Ronnie died. I mow the lawn in thirty minutes. The old mower needed a lot of work, so at the beginning of the summer I bought a new one at Home Depot. Nothing fancy. Not much of a lawn to mow—a small patch front of the house and one in the back. Half of the backyard is the patio. Laura dug out part of the lawn, placed sand and flat stones and figured how to level everything. I watched her from the window as she made mistakes and learned from them. She liked the television shows where people did things to their houses. Some of that work isn't that difficult she said it's all about having the right tools and materials. After mowing the lawn I trim the various bushes. The air has dried and cooled. Labor Day weekend is one week away. Laura's sister and brother-in-law always throw a big Labor Day party. I stopped going until Laura got sick. They never liked me. In the early days we'd argue on the way home—someone had thrown a barb at me. Laura would say it wasn't the case. But I knew what I heard. I'd catch one of her sister's eyerolls, or one of them would whisper something to the other. I stopped going. Right around the time the kids were in their mid-teens Freddy stopped going too, except maybe Thanksgiving and Christmas when I'd go. I pick up the trimmings, place them in a yard waste bag then put the clippers and mower away. On my walks, among other new additions to the downtown section of Ashford, I noticed the café. There were never many people in the place. I looked at the menu in the window. They specialized in vegetarian and healthy food. I wondered if they'd done any market research before opening in Ashford but at the same time, over the years the town has become unrecognizable. I began going to the café at the beginning of the summer. It seemed like the denizens of the place must have been reading the same books and magazines that Laura read. Up until then, I hardly ever ate out except lunch at work. Once the kids were gone, Laura went out at least once a week, with her friends, or her siblings. They'd often try different restaurants—many of them were popping up with all the new construction, houses and condominiums, strip malls. I stayed home in my room sitting up in bed watching reruns of *The Rockford Files* and *Gunsmoke*, eating frozen dinners and snacks. I order the green salad with roasted peaches and walnuts, a cup of gazpacho and an iced tea. The waitress is also the owner. Eve looks young to own a business but as the years pass my age perspective has skewed. She's got bright red hair, tattoos all over, and dressed, it seems, a bit scantily. Her eyebrows, lips and ears are pierced. The other diners in the place, male and female, are variations of Eve. They must shop from the same catalogue. I've become friendly with Eve, even developed a fatherly crush and became disheartened when I overheard conversation that she has a girlfriend. I've known few gay people. At work there were rumors about one of the managers, a single man who lived in an elegant home all by himself. I take the long way home, walking on the west side down Franklin Street then circle back along the river road. It really isn't a river—more like a stream and it never floods even in the hardest rains. Nonetheless, the Commonwealth of Massachusetts lists the Swallow River as a river. And the name's become synonymous with the names of streets, roads, developments, strip malls, auto dealerships and restaurants. I walk past The Swallow River Plaza: a pizza parlor, an insurance agency, a Chinese takeaway, a laundromat and dry-cleaners and a video store that's gone out of business. It's good to be out. In the past months there've been fleeting moments when during the morning chores, or walk, or simply at breakfast as I look out the window at a squirrel or bird— for a few moments, I feel like I'm not powerless. For several weeks after Laura died I stayed in my room except for a bathroom or kitchen run. Laura's books and magazines were strewn about the kitchen, living room and bathroom. At some point I began to look at them. I didn't read them at first—but held them and read what it said on the covers. There were articles about health, nutrition, exercise, yoga, meditation and beating cancer, or depression. I hate that word. That's what people thought about me. I know because that's what Laura said—I was depressed and maybe I could get help. I could be hard to live with and it wasn't healthy for me to come home from work every night and shut myself off from everyone. If Laura thought it, they all thought it— her family, her friends, the kids. Laura needed me sometimes. She said so. She needed my help. She needed to be loved. I read about the different meditation and relaxation techniques and learned that you didn't have to sit on the floor and meditate or do yoga—yard work and house chores and walking were also meditative activities that could help you feel better. The lifestyle and diet I'd been eating probably contributed to my fatigue, aches, pains, weight gain, sleeping problems, loss of interest in sex, loss of self-esteem, alternating between no appetite and then bingeing. It was all in the books and magazines. Deep down I knew all these things. I didn't need books to figure it out. But I wanted to relax after a long day or week at work. Comfort food and Dr Pepper helped. I'd like to have exercised but I was too tired from working all day. I wished I could socialize like other people and not be disappointed in them, or they in me.

/////

I sweep the patio and water the flowers. In Laura's gardening books I learned that some flowers last one season and others you plant return every year. I matched pictures in the books to the flowers that came up in the yard: crocus, daffodil, jonquils, iris and tulip. Red roses overgrow the trellis. Every spring Laura pruned the rosebush but I never paid attention. One morning last April, something seized me and I found the clippers and snipped the branches that looked unwieldy. Later I read that I trimmed the bush incorrectly. Branches had to be clipped at a certain angle and I'd made a straight cut. Nonetheless, I was overcome that day—a compulsion. One moment I stood in the house reaching for a Dr Pepper and the next minute I'm in the yard wielding clippers. In the days that followed, when I did some kind of chore, for a few moments it felt like I might be okay. Eventually the yard couldn't look better if Laura tended it. If only she could see me now. I should be ashamed for saying that. If Laura could see me now she'd probably ask where was I when she needed me? My father drank heavier after Ronnie died, and began spending a lot of time with Junior. The year before Junior went into the army they'd go fishing and hunting all the time. Once they drove to Boston to see the Red Sox play in Fenway Park. I preferred television—anything from a Western to a comedy show or war movie. Nothing special as long as there was something on. My mother did housework and kept herself busy. It's how she coped. Then Junior joined the army. One time I remarked to Junior that after Ronnie died everyone ignored me—like I didn't exist. Junior said I chose to go to my room and refused if asked did I want to come along. I could have been part of things but didn't want to. I fix a glass of iced sun tea. I've learned how to put a pitcher of water and tea on the windowsill and let the sun do the steeping. This batch is made with fresh mint that's overgrowing one corner of the yard. Laura planted herbs there and mint came back this spring. Last week's cooler temperatures gave way to another heat wave. I could feel it on this morning's walk. Hurricane Earl is working its way up the coast with dangerous winds. Heavy rain's expected around here. They say after the storm temperatures will drop. I drink my iced tea. Sweat beads up on my forehead and I wipe it with my forearm. Last fall Laura raked the yard and I helped her by holding open the waste bags as she filled them with dead leaves. Jan phones. She wants to say hello. I suspect she's trying to feel me out. It surprised her when I decided not to sell the house. She came right out and asked who will take care of it? I could pay someone to do it. After Laura died, Jan suggested that I buy a condominium, they're going up everywhere. I could pay cash and still have money left. She thinks I'll change my mind. I tell her I've been working on the house all summer. Her mother would be proud. She's quiet for a moment and changes the subject. Freddy is still working at a restaurant and finally rid of that crazy girlfriend though I didn't know he had a crazy girlfriend. We say goodbye let's talk soon. I open the refrigerator and stare. Six weeks since my last Dr Pepper. No processed snacks in months. I try to remember back before the kids. Everything goes fuzzy— like late in a work day, sitting at my desk watching the clock, one moment meshes with all workday moments and morphs into an incomprehensible mass of boredom. Laura and I went to the Harmony Fair on our first date. We talked but I can't recall what we said. We ate cotton candy and corn dogs and drank soda. We rode the Ferris wheel. She's laughing uncontrollably as we reel around on The Whip. I've got another doctor appointment in two weeks. Back in February I had high blood pressure, high cholesterol and forty pounds overweight. Doctor said he knew I'd been through a rough time losing Laura, but at my age, I needed to address these ailments. I've heard it for years—from Laura, from people at work, from the media, from the doctors. Cut down on meat, salt, fat, white flour. Increase fruits, vegetables and whole grains and by all means exercise. I didn't drink or smoke. In fact, I've never been fond of losing control of my faculties. The few times I tried pot it made me so paranoid that I thought people could read my mind. I've had a few too many beers a half a dozen times in my life and never liked the after-effects. So what if I liked my fried chicken dinners and

Dr Pepper? Despite what Junior, and my father, thought I didn't go to community college to avoid the service. I figured I'd sign up if I didn't get accepted at school. My grades weren't particularly good. Something about the kids that went off to college—they weren't the same when I saw them again. Many of them quit and some ended up in the war. A few of them finished and became nurses, teachers or accountants. Most people around here didn't go to college. They drove trucks, farmed part-time and worked in the trades or at one of the big companies in Brewster. My father resented me going to college. He served in the Second World War and hated communism. With a few beers he'd boast that if he were young enough, he'd gladly go over there and kill some of those slant-eyed bastards. Fact is, he knew very little about communism. No one did except me and that was only after Suzy. She liked to smoke pot and read *Walden* to me. She talked about equality, sharing and taught me about socialism. I still think about our sex, though now, I can't be certain if it really happened that way. Suzy's the reason I decided to go for social studies—until she broke my heart and I conveniently opted out of college when my father found me the job. The war is ending he said. You don't have to stay in college any more.

/////

Lately I've been thinking about sex. After a peanut butter on whole wheat, glass of soymilk and an apple, I turn on the computer to a free porn site. I never did it before. Looked at porn on the computer—until recently. I've read that diet, exercise and feeling good are related to sexual activity. Lesbian. Anal. MLF. Teen. Group. I haven't had real sex in twenty years. A winter Sunday afternoon, the kids—gone, somewhere. Laura initiated things. We started kissing and touching and in my usual fashion I got on top. When we finished and lay there it began to snow—one of the biggest storms that winter. I suspected that Laura had been with her friend Henry so I got close to Margaret at the office. Divorced, Margaret had two kids and made it clear to me that she could be available though I wasn't the first person to whom Margaret made herself available. We never went all the way but a few nights we stayed in the office late and mugged it up. She said she could make me very happy. That we could go to her place any time her children were staying with their father. But I was always at work or in my room. To be anywhere else I'd have to tell Laura a lie. And I'd surely get caught. Margaret moved on to a regional manager. I step off the scale fifteen pounds lighter than four months ago. In the beginning I resented the morning stretches and walks but felt compelled to move. I used to rush. These days I take my time enjoy to the birds and the sounds of the world. I plan my lunch and dinner as I go. Most of my life I ate out of the frozen food section. Now it's produce and health foods. Other than Jan and the owner of the café, I haven't had a conversation with anyone since May when the man came out to change the gas meter. We talked about Iraq where his brother was stationed and his little brother on the way. There's nothing you can do with these people he said—it's in their bible to kill us, and kill our children too. What kind of crazy religion is that? He had three kids, two with a first wife, one with his second. Lately I've tried to start up a conversation with a cashier at the market, a Chinese woman but I only seem to hold up the line. Most of my life, I've tried to avoid human contact. The moment I don't absolutely have to be somewhere, I want my space. Now, I feel antsy, almost as if I'd like to talk to someone. My neighbors are having a party in the yard behind me. They've been living there for several years. We've never really said hello. The wife's Asian and her husband a white guy. Over the years, more people of different color and creed have moved to the area. An Indian family lives on our street. Blacks and Hispanics have moved into Ashford. The people behind me are cooking. I smell meat and hear more voices in the air as new guests arrive. They built the house fifteen years ago when the road was cut in from Route 115. Until then, it was woods back there where deer, small animals and birds lived. During the construction of all the houses windows were broken and some equipment damaged. Freddy and some friends got taken in for vandalism. The police said there were signs of drinking but they wouldn't pursue that. The boys confessed but it cost us and we had to contribute to the damages. I always took one day at a time because if I looked at the big picture— of all those days and years ahead, having to get up, go to work, week in and week out—I panicked. It was hard enough each morning when the alarm struck and I opened my eyes to the realization of going to work. Laura made her own life and when the kids got older she got a job at the Shoe Outlet. It was only twenty-four hours a week but she became a part-time supervisor. That's where she met Henry. She always maintained they were work friends. He had a wife and three kids. I sensed something in the way she spoke about him. They were on the Shoe Outlet's bowling team and Laura never bowled until then. She claimed her co-workers coaxed her into it and after bowling everyone went for pizza and beer. I sweep and mop the kitchen floor, wipe down the counters and appliances then vacuum the living room. I try to imagine Laura doing all the chores every day and taking care of the kids and dropping them off somewhere and picking them up and grocery shopping and laundry and cooking. Years seem unaccountable— kids in diapers, Laura cooking suppers, my drives back and forth to work, Jan riding a horse, Freddy getting his girlfriend pregnant, Christmas mornings, my father dying, my mother dying, Ronnie dying. I try to recall one concrete incident from a day at my job but things blur. I remember one afternoon Suzy and I drove all the way to Walden Pond in Concord. We smoked pot and Suzy had to drive home because I was too high. Exactly what year was that? What day? What season? Early on the job I discovered the daily workload in the division offices to be three hours to four hours. The rest—walks to the cooler, walks to the bathroom, walks to the snack room, talking with co-workers who were always ready for gossip or rehashed television barbs. I became office manager in charge of eight people. Over the years with budget cuts, it was gradually reduced until the office consisted of me and one office assistant. Even then the workload was nominal. The office was eliminated when I took early retirement. I sit out on the patio with Laura's book on herbs and their healing properties. People have been using them for thousands of years. Some medications in modern Western medicine can be traced to chemicals in ancient healing potions. I look over at the folks in the yard. Kids run and play. Adults gather around a large table eating and drinking, talking and laughing. The woman who owns the house catches me looking, and smiles. I smile back. I don't much like the book on herbs. It reads like a dry textbook. I close it, lock up the house and decide to take a ride. The car's been sitting idle for weeks. I haven't used it for anything. All my errands are done on foot. I drive through town and get on 115 towards Harmony. I don't intend on going to Laura's family's Labor Day party but I steer the car right past the house and slow down to see the cars parked out front and people gathered in the backyard. Jenny called for the Fourth of July party and invited me. She said I was always welcome at any of their annual parties. On the way back I stop at the market to get something to eat. It is the holiday after all. I'm entitled to a special treat. Everyone's eating burgers, dogs, steaks, chicken, cookies, ice cream let alone all the booze. Can I go to the deli section and pick up some precooked ribs or a whole roasted chicken, just this day? I opt for veggie burgers. Used to be I had the television on every waking hour. Sometimes I'd leave it on all night. Now I watch mostly in the evening, when the day's winding down. I catch an old movie or a rerun of one of my old favorites *The Rockford Files*, *Mission Impossible* or *Bonanza*. I never noticed before how much I dislike commercials. Maybe it's because I want to avoid salty snacks or Hungry Man dinners and soda. Since commandeering the kitchen in the spring, I began using the living room. I never went so far as sit in Laura's plush recliner, my Christmas gift to her the year before she died. I couldn't sit in it. And I couldn't sell it. I did, however, buy my own recliner and set it right next to hers.

/////

I found the dildo on the day the insurance check arrived. In April, clearing things out of Laura's closet I discovered the flesh-colored object under blankets in a box. It didn't make sense. I couldn't put Laura and the dildo together. It couldn't be hers. Why would she have left it there? Over the next few days I agonized over the dildo. I cancelled an appointment scheduled with a money manager. The news travels fast, I quickly realized, no sooner did Laura die people began contacting me saying they were in the business of helping me protect my money. I know nothing about such matters and how to manage my money. Besides the kids, I don't know anyone I can call on about anything. Laura always handled the finances. I never paid a bill and Laura continued to pay them nearly to the end. Only recently I learned how to do things online. Most of that came from calling the numbers on the help lines, waiting for long periods of time, and eventually getting a human on the other end who would guide me through the process.

I couldn't imagine Laura using the dildo. What did she do with it? I left it on the middle of Laura's bed. One night I sat on the edge of the bed, unzipped my pants and began stroking while looking at the dildo. Outside the wind swirled rattling the gutters and eaves. A trash can turned over. I imagined Laura using the toy and even thought of Laura using the dildo on me. I reached and brought it closer for a look readying to finish then brought the dildo down to my testicles and pressed the tip lightly against the base of the scrotum. I came on my stomach and the bedspread. For a few moments I lay there gasping for air then rolled to the side and studied the dildo. I sat up to my reflection in Laura's bedroom mirror—fat, homely, old and balding—masturbating with my dead wife's dildo. I wash the car. The water from the hose is cold. At night temperatures have been dropping into the forties and fifties. On my walks I wear a jacket. The plush towel feels good as I massage it around to dry the car. I shake out the floor mats and clean the inside windows and dashboard. Laura left a box full of tools that contained all I need to do minor work on the car so I went online and found it's easy to change my own oil and I feel better doing it myself. For years I simply drove the car. Never went to a car wash. The interior was littered with fast food wrappers, empty Dr Pepper cans, bottles and crumpled chip bags. The inside windows had a layer of soot. I rarely serviced our cars. If they broke down, I'd have them fixed. Once I went three years without changing the oil. When I finish cleaning the car I fix lunch—spinach salad with tuna fish on top, a banana and glass of pomegranate juice. Seems like I eat one meal and start thinking about the next. Most afternoons I walk to the market for dinner groceries. A car door slams next door. I go to the living room window to peek through the blind. The Coviello's have lived there for twenty years and I never conversed with either of them. They're a few years younger than us. Laura got friendlier with them when she was dying and they attended her wake. Mrs. Coviello knocked on our door a day or two later with a dish of pasta and meatballs and said if I needed anything to let her or her husband know. From behind the curtain I watch her walk around the car, up the stairs and onto the deck. She's shapely. I wonder if she and Mr. Coviello still get around to it. There were times when I accepted the fact that I might never have sex again. Since it's been more than twenty years it means nearly half my adult life. I can't get my mind off Mrs. Coviello. At the market I keep thinking about her and grow flustered and hurry home to put the groceries away then go to the living room and masturbate. Mrs. Coviello and I end up alone doing different things to each other and she's using Laura's dildo on herself. Suddenly at the last instant I think of Helen. During the summer on my visits to the market, I began to wander to her aisle to cash out, even if other cashiers had less of a backup. Her nametag read Helen. She spoke English with a Chinese accent. Once or twice I've attempted a short conversation but invariably there are people behind me in the line. She's plain and beautiful. In this way, she reminds me of Laura—no make-up, glowing skin. Laura had spirited eyes and oversized thighs she fought against her entire life—running and walking and dieting. I rather liked them. I overheard Helen in a conversation with other

25

customers speaking about a son who lives in New York. On my way home from the market I stop at the café for an iced tea. The lunch crowd's thinned out and I'm the only patron besides a young man with long hair and his eyebrows and lip pierced. He and Eve are discussing the idea of an open mic night at the café. I don't understand what they mean but after eavesdropping it sounds like musicians can come in, sign up and play two songs. He says the open mics have been very successful and it would be a good way to fill the café with people on slow nights during the week. Eve seems enthused and tells him she'll give it a try. They settle on Tuesdays. I've never been interested in music, but maybe some Tuesday night I'll check it out. Laura made occasional attempts to broach the subject of our problems. She said that she felt I was withdrawn and unavailable—that she needed me emotionally and physically, that my negativity could be hard to take. But there was nothing wrong with me. I worked hard all day and had a right to spend my down time any way I pleased. I didn't like people and didn't want to spend my valuable time with them. Then one day Laura told me she didn't care about sex with me any more. That she'd hoped for a long time we could enjoy each other again but it was clear that I had no interest. She began going out more, with relatives, friends and then who knows after Henry. And then there was the dildo. Freddy phones. If he's calling, he needs something. I figure he wants money and since I have some now, I'll give it to him. The last thing I expect is Freddy asking, can he move home for a short time? I flash on a passage in a book Laura highlighted—how people get into the same patterns and keep repeating things unable to end unhealthy cycles. I didn't want Freddy back but I had no choice. No drinking in the house I say. And he must find a job right away. Freddy says it will be a brief stay, he already has a job lined up and more importantly he's not drinking. He has a long history of screwing up, but I can't say no.

/////

I moved out of my parents' house second year at community college. My father didn't understand why I'd waste money on rent when we lived half an hour away from the school. I shared an apartment in Brewster with two other guys and got a part-time job at Sears and Roebuck working in the warehouse. Everywhere around me people were letting loose—guys growing their hair long, girls throwing away bras, kids talked about serious things like the war and making a better world while smoking pot and taking acid. What happened all of a sudden? I felt estranged from it all and wore my hair short and parted on the side the way I did as a boy. Talk of revolution confused me. I never owned any record albums, not even the Beatles. I knew nothing about Viet Nam. My father served in the army in the Second World War—that war was black and white—Hitler had to be stopped and the Japanese attacked Pearl Harbor. Suzy played lots of records, smoked pot and said everything will be better when it's our world. She told me that every person in China had free education, health care and a job. Something about being with Suzy made me feel good—and she was the first. Up to then I'd only done touch and feel stuff with my senior prom date. I went last minute. Her name was Denise we chatted a bit in history class and somehow ended up at the prom. But Suzy was something else—experienced and free in a way I had never known in a woman to be. I can't say I'm excited about Freddy moving back. I've grown fond of the daily rituals—rising, stretching, walking, breakfast, morning chores, lunch, afternoon walk to the market, supper. I like washing the dishes by hand, wiping down the table and counters and sweeping the kitchen floor. Freddy will be an intruder. I'll have to set limits. Laura once said as far as our relationship went, the final straw came when she asked me for help with Freddy when he started having serious problems. I did nothing. I figured he'd straighten out. Helen tallies the groceries. How are you? Good, she says. Hoping for conversation so I tell her my son's coming home. There's no one else in line I can stall. She smiles and says that's nice. I don't know what to say next. Is she a widower? Traditional Chinese woman, I imagine, wouldn't be divorced. Well, it's a beautiful day do you have to work all day? Four o'clock. Ah good I reply, still time to enjoy it. Suddenly a woman with two kids and a full grocery cart appears. Time to move. My father and Junior built the tree house. Junior had an idea that he would sleep up there and shoot a deer at first dawn. He never did. I used it more than anyone. The wooden box frame nestled in the fork of a great maple became a haven. A few times one summer Ronnie and I slept up there but the mosquitoes drove us into the house. I hid away for hours, mostly doing nothing in the woods behind our house, cut off from the outside. I watched squirrels and chipmunks, tiny field mice, moles, rabbits and birds of every sort. Scurrying animals could be heard along the ground, the innumerable birdcalls and the chipping of red squirrels. Once, I saw a doe and her fawn feeding. I saw a big buck and a silver fox too. Sometimes I masturbated. The first finance person I spoke with was a woman. Found her online. Most of them are men but Maureen Stanley had her picture posted and looked young and attractive. Over the course of two hours she explained my various options. Laura's insurance check, my monthly retirement and social security combined with the net worth of the house is more money than I've ever known. While Maureen talked I snuck glimpses of her, prettier in person than the photograph—blonde hair, make-up and hint of cleavage didn't hurt although I've never been attracted to the flashy types. Laura was pretty but in a natural way. She never dressed too showy though when her hair went gray she colored it. She always said I'm most comfortable wearing jeans and a sweatshirt. I couldn't make sense of anything Maureen said. She looked at me and smiled between her explanations asking are you getting some of this? It became a little game and for a moment, I fantasized that we were flirting. She left warning that I didn't have much time to get my finances in order and she'd be in touch. I told her to drive carefully as the roads were icy from a late spring storm. She called me once a week until I let her be the one to handle the finances. I bring the attic stuff that I'd stored in Freddy's room to the garage. Freddy played little league baseball for a couple of years and on Saturday mornings we attended some of the games. Laura got passionate about it and shouted at the players and coaches and empires. I remained indifferent. Laura got to know all the other parents while I hung in the background avoiding contact as much as possible. She rarely had a bad thing to say about anyone. Nobody's perfect and everybody has faults. That's what she said. We met at a wedding. At the reception a female cousin approached and said I must meet her friend Laura. I was still reeling from the loss of Suzy. I still loved her. We made small talk. I sensed that she wanted to dance because every time the band played a song she said this is a good song. I had never danced in my life. Later Laura taught me a few basic steps and once or twice we danced at a wedding. One by one the relatives of my generation got married, then the kids started popping out. At gatherings, people said things like where does the time go? I began to avoid as many social events as I could. I didn't like petty talk. People sensed that about me and thought me a snob. I didn't want to talk about my job—I detested it. I didn't want to hear about their jobs. I didn't want to hear about their kids or what they did on summer vacations. Ronnie and I shared one bedroom. We slept in a bunk bed. Me up Ronnie down. My parents were in the second bedroom, and Junior slept in the small bedroom. Ronnie was a chubby baby and my mother said that when she breastfed him he drank more milk than her other boys combined. Being fat made him a bit of an outcast at school. He and I mostly hung together. We sat next to each other on the school bus and played together after school. Despite his physical shape, Ronnie loved to play baseball and hockey. Occasionally he'd drag me down the field to hit some balls, or in winter we skated on Miller's Pond and shot a hockey puck around. I was slow and clumsy when it came to sports. Ronnie improved and eventually sports became his door to social acceptance. Junior, always the star, gloated over his little brother. Ronnie became a catcher and a solid hitter. I was in my room when the police came to the door. That somebody can just be gone like that. Forever. Night after night I lay in bed unable to sleep, crying, cursing and disavowing God. In time, my mother pretended it never happened. She would sometimes speak of Ronnie as if he were in the next room. She'd be cooking beef stew. You know your brother loves beef stew, referring to Ronnie. You know your brother always loves to watch the Sox play the Yankees. You know your brother never misses opening day of the deer season.

/////

I rake the newly fallen leaves wondering how many more times I'll have to mow the lawn before first frost. During the day the sun still warms things up and perennials continue to produce. A door closes and Mrs. Coviello walks down the stairs to her car and drives away. Mr. Coviello hasn't aged as well as his wife. Just yesterday I noticed his belly and he's lost most of his hair. I remembered when their kids were young and still lived at home. When Freddy came to town for Laura's funeral, he appeared to be sober and stayed at the house for a few days. With the commotion and so many people around we hardly spoke. I had guests over the house after the service—Laura's family, three generations of them and her many friends. Over the years they all knew about our marriage, or at least Laura's version. I had food catered and Laura's sisters took care of putting everything out and stayed to help clean up. At the service they spoke about Laura, that she loved life, that she was a great mother and friend—

33

always there when you needed her. When I open the door Freddy attempts a hug but I stiffen so he places his hand on my shoulder. I look good he says new diet? I launch into a brief explanation of changing my eating habits, the walks and daily chores. If Laura could see me now he says bringing his bags to the bedroom. I ask can I get him anything? A cup of coffee but I only have tea. Freddy says he'll pick some up he drinks a lot of it these days. I've planned a trip to the market and tell him to come along and pick up anything he needs. He insists that he drive rather than walk. I try to persuade him but he wins out. Freddy got his license back six months ago, and he's been working at a restaurant and making enough money to buy a used car. I assumed he'd been fired from his most recent job and probably gone off the wagon. But Freddy says he worked up to sous-chef. I don't know what sous-chef means and he explains that it's first under the chef. He's here because he found a sous-chef position in a new restaurant opening in Brewster. It's a better opportunity and he knows the manager from a previous job. The manager is also in recovery. He won't let me pay for anything at the market. I had planned on some fish, maybe brown rice and a simple salad. I tell him I don't eat meat any more not even chicken. He runs around the produce section poking and picking vegetables, lifting things up to examine them. At the fish counter, he walks up to the glass, looks long and decides on scallops. He's impressed when I tell him all the herbs and spices I have at home. I lead the way to the cash-out counter looking for Helen. She's in number six. This is my son I say as she rings the items. Helen looks at Freddy and says hello. On the way home he explains he's been sober for over a year—more or less. He slipped a couple of times early on but hasn't had a drink since Laura died. It's not that he made any vows or anything like that. It just seemed to happen that way. He goes to meetings, often every day. At times he still feels that he needs and deserves a drink. But somehow he's made it through one crisis at a time. I couldn't recall exactly when Freddy became a chef. I never remember him boiling a hot dog. After years of various jobs Freddy began working in restaurants. He cooks pan-seared scallops with an Asian glaze and says that he's reconciled with his ex-wife and visiting with my granddaughter whom I haven't seen in fifteen years. Along with the scallops he serves crispy noodles and spicy sautéed greens. We talk, catch up. About Jan, about his newfound success as a chef, about being retired and all the work I've been doing around the house. This morning he didn't want to walk with me. You go, I don't care much for walking he said. Besides, he didn't want to interrupt my special routine. But I insisted and he gave in. Along the river road ducks quack and fly overhead, on the move this time of year. In town we pass the new café on Main Street. From inside Eve waves and I wave back. We go in the café for coffee. At times I've admitted to myself that some of what Laura said wasn't so far off the mark. That hiding in my room at night and not wanting to take part in anything might not be the healthiest thing. But I felt that way as long as I could remember— even before Ronnie died. I preferred to be left alone. Other kids seemed dull and silly. At school a day never passed without my being the brunt of someone's or a group's disapproval. I don't know why I feel compelled to share this information with Freddy now, but as we sit in the café, Freddy drinking a second espresso and me slowly sipping a pot of green tea, it seems to come out naturally. As office manager I had to socialize with co-workers on occasion—a retirement party or the annual Christmas party. It was the aspect of the job I hated most. I'd have to say a few words and make a toast. I envy people who can do special things—a fine carpenter, an artist, even a mechanic who can tune an engine to perfection. Nothing ever appealed enough for me to make the effort. I often wondered what I might have done—had I not taken the job and instead finished my college education—had I not married Laura—had I started exercising and eating better ten or twenty years ago—had I gone with Ronnie the night he died. After leaving, I never moved back into my parents' house. The freedom that came from having my own space was worth working two jobs. Later, my salary from the state kept me afloat. I had a few roommates most of whom I ignored then met and married Laura in what now seems like ten minute's time. Kids partied when I was young. Most of them turned out all right. I figured Freddy would too but when it became time for turning around Freddy got arrested the first time. Jan lost interest in riding and we sold her horse to pay the lawyer. It seemed like a lot of money then. I disliked jocks more than anyone— more than the hippies or the hicks. The better athlete that Ronnie became, the further apart he and I grew. He wanted me to go with him that night. It would be good to get out, and there were girls. I said they didn't like me and I didn't fit in. He said that's what you think but it's not that way and his friends were nice guys. He urged me to go to the party—it was Saturday night and I shouldn't spend it sitting in the room. Finally he became impatient and said stay home and sulk. If you weren't good at sports you'd be a fat joke to them. Those were my last words to him.

/////

I told Freddy stay as long as you need but he's got an apartment lined up in Brewster first of the month. He asked what got me into the walking and healthy eating and I told him about Laura's books and magazines—how one thing just led to the next. I dream about her almost every night. Laura's death brought me back to Ronnie's death, and the startling fact that suddenly, randomly, people get taken away. I know that we all die but why those before their time? In one book I read that you die when it's your time to die and who's to say who lives a bad life in a hundred years or a great life in sixteen? I stopped believing in God when Ronnie died. Laura said she wasn't sure about God but went along mostly for the kids, she thought children needed something to believe in. I still get cravings for Dr Pepper, fried chicken or potato chips. The longer I stay away the less the cravings come. Freddy says he wants to drink every day. Some days it's easier than others. But any night he goes to bed sober he's grateful. He's sorry he says for all the problems he caused but I interrupt I should be the one apologizing. I should have done something to help Freddy when he was young but I failed him, and Laura. He says he's hurt a lot of people including his own daughter. The one person he should have made right with was his mother and now it's too late. He's off to Brewster the restaurant opens in two weeks he says there's lots to do. I sweep the patio and driveway. Freddy made it through high school and then worked several uninteresting jobs—the warehouse of a paper company, driving a delivery van and working at the 7-Eleven. During the Gulf War, he joined the army. He already had a problem by then. In high school he hid booze in his locker. By the time he finished basic training the war ended and he spent most of his stint in Europe. His daughter lives with her mother in New Hampshire. Freddy owed her alimony and she got it attached to his military check. He came back from the army aimless as when he went in and the drinking reached another level. I put the broom away and fix a spinach salad with crushed walnuts and a bit of blue cheese. I've impressed Freddy with my culinary skills. When he got out of the army we let him move back into the house. There were a few jobs but nothing panned out. His drinking began to spill over into the household. He'd come home drunk and loud and if Laura or I tried to speak with him he became argumentative and belligerent. Sometimes when he drank he reminded me of my father—he'd repeat himself and get hostile. Then he lost his license again. There were days when he tried not to drink and went out to look for a job. But day after day ended the same and eventually he remained in his room drinking alone. Laura, Jan and I had cut Freddy off. We didn't know where he got his booze money and learned not to leave valuables around because Freddy would help himself. Laura pleaded with me to help her with Freddy. She went to meetings for people related to alcoholics and wanted me to go along but I wouldn't. Why couldn't she go and tell me what they said? It didn't work that way. If she and I didn't help him, he'd be lost. If he wants to stop, he has to do it himself I insisted and my going to meetings wouldn't help. The night Laura called the police was the first of many last chances. I tried to calm Freddy down and Freddy got in my face, calling me a loser and pushing me, threatening to punch me in the nose. Laura tried to intervene and Freddy shoved her aside. I grabbed him and we wrestled to the kitchen floor. Jan was screaming call the police they're going to kill each other. At first, Laura and I were going to press charges. Let him bottom out Laura said. If he has to spend a couple of days in jail, it might be just what he needs. After the talking with the officer, we decided against it. But we gave Freddy two weeks to move out. There was a beaver pond in the woods behind our house. Ronnie and I fished in the spring when streams rose and beaver dams backed up the waterways. We caught brook trout using worms on hooks. Sometimes the beaver swam at us trying to scare us off the dam. The dam would weaken from our weight, and water poured over the sides where it shouldn't. When we wore out one section of the dam, we moved on to another. I feared that the dam would cave in and I might drown in the aftermath. Sometimes I stayed on solid ground and watched Ronnie fish while I swatted the swarms of mosquitoes. The trout were small, usually five or six inches with delicious orange flesh and we brought them home where our mother fried them heads on in bacon fat and we'd eat them with eggs and bacon. Ronnie caught the most. I often had gear problems and tangles—or overcast my mark so the hook would land in a tree on the other side of the tiny pond. And I hated the mosquitoes no matter how much rank Woodsman's Oil I rubbed on my skin. I couldn't keep them away. Ronnie fished hard he never seemed to mind the bugs. Yesterday morning Freddy took me to Brewster to show me the restaurant and introduced me to the chef. It's quite a fancy place. Not the Brewster I remember. Things have to change Freddy said, it's part of the bigger picture. Then he brought me to see his new apartment—a one bedroom with a big living room and modern kitchen. You used to get an apartment in Brewster for less than a hundred bucks a month. He's seeing his daughter regularly again. I told him he's doing a great job and if it means anything to him I'm proud of how he turned things around. We stopped to eat at a Thai restaurant. I ordered pad thai but Freddy said that's not what you want and ordered for the both of us—a delicate seafood soup with vegetables and noodles. Tonight he didn't come home when he should. I think about phoning him but decide not. The stir-fry with brown rice is cold. If Freddy knew he'd be late, why not call? He's drinking. It couldn't be anything else or he would have phoned. I call his cell. It rings and switches to message. I hang up. What if he tries to drive? How could he put himself at such risk? I put the leftover stir-fry in the fridge, clean the table and counters, wash the dishes then sweep the floor. I can't remember when I stopped using the machine there's something about hand washing the bowls, dishes, pans and utensils three times a day after eating. I'm angry and guilty because part of me expected this to happen and it did. I remember his words about how if you do slip you have to get up the next day and start over again. I sit down and pick up one of Laura's books, about achieving harmony and balance through focusing on what is real, not what you imagine. That's what it says in the jacket. We must gradually shed the artificial in order to see what's really shining. I can't concentrate. I almost phone him again. There's nothing else it could be—otherwise he would have called. Suddenly his car pulls in the driveway and I pretend to read when he comes in, playing it cool and sizing up his condition. I flash on the ugly nights of years past, and Laura and Jan and it sickens me to think that maybe things don't change after all. Maybe a year from now I'll be sitting in front of the television eating fried chicken. He's sorry he didn't call he got tied up with a problem at work and two hours flew by like a minute. After that he sat down for a quick bite with the chef and manager. What have I been up to he wants to know? He's tired after a long day and goes to bed. Got a lot more long ones ahead he says on the way. When I return from my morning walk he's ready to leave for work. Time for coffee I ask? He's got to go he says, lots of things to iron out before the opening. Then he invites me to the opening. Who would be there? All sorts of people and it will be good for me to get out. He saw that I called last night, was anything up? He must know what I didn't want him to know, that I thought he'd been drinking.

Just called to check in before I put your dinner in the refrigerator. When you didn't pick up I figured you must have been busy so I didn't leave a message. I don't really want to go to the opening. The only person I'll know is Freddy and he'll be in the kitchen cooking. He says there'll be restaurant people, friends and family of employees, a few people from the local culinary press, business people and maybe a politician or two. I can sit at the bar and he'll send me delicacies from the kitchen. I prefer the company of strangers to people I know so maybe it won't be such a bad idea. I can't remember the last time I've been to a nice restaurant or sat at a bar. It isn't that I like strangers—they're like everybody else once you get to know them.

/////

Temperatures drop from tropical to near freezing in a few days, knocking down most of the perennials. Within a week leaves turn gold, yellow, orange and red. Today Freddy moves to his own apartment. I fantasized about us living in the house together—two bachelors. Freddy's daughter could come and visit though I hardly know her she's nearly a grown woman. I've got used to him being around. He suggested I buy a snowblower, but this year I look forward to the shoveling and already purchased a new shovel at Home Depot. When Laura first told me about her cancer, I asked her what it meant. A malignant tumor was growing inside and she explained the details using words about a woman's inside parts I'd heard about but never fully understood. Surgery would be immediate, followed by chemotherapy. There were various scenarios. They might cut her open and find more cancer than previously thought, close her up and send her home to die. They might get it all and with chemo, she could live, possibly, for many years. I'd just learned I had to take early retirement. Could it kill her? It might, but she wouldn't go down easy she said. The surgery went as well as hoped, and it looked as if they got all the cancer. I took her to chemotherapy sessions and went to the pharmacist for her prescriptions learning the names and uses of each of medication. Laura grew weak and experienced ferocious bouts of nausea. She was a model patient. Soon as she recovered she went back to her newfound regiment of a plant-based diet and exercise. She'd always been active and ate well but now was convinced diet and exercise were key to her future. I watched as she biked, hiked, walked and practiced yoga in the middle of the living room. She experimented with cooking grains and all varieties of beans, legumes, vegetables and tofu. She made smoothies in the blender with fresh fruit. Over time, I noticed that Laura's shape had returned to the way she looked before she had children. Her skin shone newfound light. Occasionally Laura tried to coax me into taking a walk or eating a stir-fry and rice, but I kept with my old favorites. Laura carried on as if she'd never been sick. That period of time passed dreamily for me, when Laura seemed to have beat it, and returned to her life, family, friends. I think coming so close to death gave her a newfound energy. She began to radiate. I stayed close to home watching Laura come and go with her fresh verve but I never wandered far from my room and old routines. I couldn't tell whether early retirement was a curse or a blessing. Laura and I grew friendlier towards each other though we spoke sparingly, mostly news about the kids or household related business. I can't finish the stir-fried noodles that I made. I don't have much of an appetite—I miss Freddy. I wash the dishes, pans, sweep the floor and wipe the table and counters. It's good I'll go to the opening. After all the times I let Freddy down it's time I supported him. Laura would. I pick up a book skim over sections but pay attention to where Laura highlighted passages or wrote margin notes. One chapter has to do with people who hide themselves behind doors, sit with regretful or blameful minds, what a self-limiting practice that becomes. On the other hand, those who are out in the world, mixing and keeping open minds are likely to live more fulfilling lives. I've never found people special in any way. It isn't that I think I'm better—they simply bore me and make me uncomfortable. And I know others have always considered me dull. When the kids were young during the first week of August we went camping. Laura's family reserved the same camp sites at a state park and pitched their tents and set up house. When Laura's family gathered like that, it seemed to me that family members were slight variations of the same person. It was like one big mass of them. They were their own biggest fans, forever boasting about themselves or their children or their pasts. The men told fishing and hunting stories and the women spoke of pregnancies and kids. They drank beer, coffee and Kool Aid. They ate bacon-and-egg breakfasts, hot dogs and hamburgers afternoon and night. The kids swam in the lake and played their kid vacation games. Parents sat around picnic tables under gas lamplight late into the night playing cards, smoking and drinking beer. Red Sox games aired on portable radios. I didn't play cards and didn't follow the baseball games. I did like to swim.

Never able to sleep well on an air mattress, I usually woke before anyone, slipped into my swim trunks and swam with the lake to myself, often in the morning fog before the rising sun had burned it off. It was the only pleasure I took on those vacations. The year it rained all week turned out to be the last camping trip we took together. All that rain and nowhere to go. Everyone gathered under two big tarps. The firewood got damp and difficult to burn. Smoke blew recklessly around us. Rain soaked through tents and dripped on us as we tried to sleep. Arguments broke out between couples, between siblings and cousins. Freddy and his cousin Johnny had a bottle of whisky. One day they snuck off to the woods to drink and got lost. They were wandering on a road drenched and drunk when a ranger picked them up. Laura accused me of being anti-social. I barely spoke to anyone. Couldn't I at least be part of a conversation? We left for home a day early. The next year Freddy said that he didn't want to go camping. I offered to stay home with Freddy and Laura and Jan went without us. I hear the geese but can't see them above the fog-covered river. My father hunted geese. He had an old rowboat painted camouflage used for fishing and waterfowl shooting. He'd row on the marshes, set out decoys, call ducks and geese in and bang. Like most people in the area we ate a lot of game. In the fall, there were rabbits, pheasants, waterfowl and venison in the freezer during winter. Home from my walk I rake the leaves in the front and back. Many have fallen in the recent rain and winds. I rake into neat piles then scoop them into yard waste bags. I catch sight of Mrs. Coviello's car coming down the far end of the street. Rather than go right into the house I linger. As she pulls into the driveway I walk to my front door. She steps out of the car and smiles. I smile with a gentle wave. Lunch is leftover salmon and spinach salad. The test results arrived with a note from the doctor saying that my cholesterol had dropped, the rest of my blood work came back normal, and it was good to see my blood pressure down. Everything I had read seemed true. Eat the right things, be active and you'll be healthier and feel better. Suddenly a chilly wave swept through me. What was this new life? I rose at six drank a cup of green tea, stretched and walked three miles. All my life I set the alarm for the last possible minute that I could safely get to work on time—7:17 A.M. I drank my first mug of coffee and did my should-or-shouldn't-I-call-in-sick-tug-of-war while I dressed. But if it were true about the diet and exercise being so important, why did Laura die? At the opening Freddy finds me a seat at the bar and introduces me to the bartender, a young woman named Rebecca. He disappears into the kitchen. I don't know what to order then settle on a glass of red wine at Rebecca's suggestion. It's crowded and the owners and managers mingle with all the people. Freddy comes and goes bringing me tidbits to eat. Every time I finish something Rebecca arrives with a big smile asks how did I like that? I'm the sole loner at the crowded bar. Most folks are gathered in groups around stools. Laura and I didn't eat out often. When we did we went to Kitty's Steak House. It wasn't fancy. Laura wore her hooded sweatshirt and jeans. They cooked good steaks and had spaghetti and the kids liked it. Sometimes we went there on Sunday afternoons in lieu of Laura cooking a roast. Freddy asks could I take another course or ready for dessert? I can't eat anything else but Freddy returns with chocolate mousse and says take an extra long walk tomorrow. The glass of wine and rich food make me feel bloated and tipsy. It's the first drink I've had since a beer the day we buried Laura. I just want to be home and curled up in bed. More people crowd into the bar. Occasionally I catch Rebecca's eye and she smiles. I must look like a real loser sitting here alone. Next time I see Freddy I let him know I'm going soon. I congratulate him again and ask about the new apartment. Everything's going great and he thanks me for coming. I beckon a busy Rebecca and ask for a check. She says I don't have a check tonight. I think I should leave her a tip but not certain how much. I am the sous-chef's father after all. I take out a ten then put it back for a twenty. As I leave the nearby group spills over the empty stool. In the morning, the heater turns on automatically. I didn't sleep well. My stomach was rumbling and my mind energized by the excitement at the restaurant. I worry that I haven't changed the filter on the furnace. There are several trips to the bathroom. Fatigued, I struggle to get out of bed and decide to sleep in. Why not do as I please? When I retired, my greatest pleasure was to stop setting the alarm. Years ago I could stay in bed until eleven on weekend mornings. I toss and turn feeling guilty for not stretching and taking a walk like I should, especially after all the food last night. Nothing appeals to me at breakfast—not fruit, yogurt, cereal, toast, soymilk or tea. I decide to take myself out for breakfast and drive to town to the café, but my tastes are for something more traditional and I go to Denny's for pancakes, eggs and home fries. The waitress asks no meat? I almost order a side of sausage but decide against it. I eat everything on my plate and put butter and jelly on the toast. It's the first cup of coffee in months. After eating I'm anxious and have stomach cramps and heartburn. I don't want to change the filter on the furnace or mop the kitchen floor and vacuum like I planned today. Nor do I wish to walk to the market later. I spend the morning in front of the television, switching channels. There's a show on the Old West, game shows, reality shows, home shows, cooking shows, sports shows, news channels, movies and reruns of old situation comedies including an old favorite *The Andy Griffith Show*. I try to convince myself that I can take a day off if I want I've been good for a long time and deserve some time to relax, do nothing and eat a little outside the norm. I flash on the people at the opening last night, the bits and pieces of conversation overheard—sports, kids, jobs, relationships. A cold can of Dr Pepper sounds good to me. I drive to the market for a six-pack of it, a frozen chicken dinner and a bag of salt and vinegar potato chips avoiding Helen at her checkout line for the ten items or less express.

/////

I force myself out of bed, stretch and walk. Two days
off the old regiment turned me sluggish. Once out, I
can only think about getting home so I walk faster and
lose my breath. My stomach burns from the bad food—
the soda, chips, chicken dinner, the greasy breakfast. I
haven't taken a healthy shit in two mornings. Worse—
an all too familiar helplessness descends. My throat feels
sore. Laura spent countless hours driving Jan back and
forth to the barn, and to horse events. She'd let Freddy
and his friends hang out on weekend nights and make
pizza for them until they began sneaking booze in. She
put in hours after school with Freddy, tutoring him so
he could graduate. With the money from her job she
started a fund for the kids' college tuition. Freddy never
went to college but she later gave him money for cooking
school. Laura did their laundry, bought groceries and
cooked meals until each moved out of the house. She
went to PTA meetings and met with teachers, attended
school talent and holiday shows. She went alone to meet

with the school principal when Freddy got suspended. She put up Christmas decorations, took the kids to pick out the tree and did holiday shopping. I feel a little better having changed the filter on the furnace. It's not complicated but a task I fear nonetheless. I mop the kitchen floor and vacuum the living room. Suddenly I'm drawn to my room and look under the bed for the bag containing Laura's dildo. I place it on the bed. What did Laura do with it? Did she have lovers other than Henry? Did she have some kind of secret lesbian life? For a while it seemed that some kind of sex drive had returned. It took me a while to get there, but things were successful. As the season has changed that seems to have been lost. The few times I've tried, even with Internet help, nothing. Laura always wore jeans and a sweatshirt—and pitched a mean softball in her family's annual Guys vs. Gals game. I put the dildo back in the bag and slip it under the bed. Since the opening I've been trying to fight back thoughts of death—Laura's, Ronnie's, my parents', my own. What if I get a disease that takes a while to kill me? I'll die alone. I watched her close her eyes for the last time and breathe her last breath. It must have made it easier for her in the end— to have me around the house, run errands and drive her to doctor appointments. I could have spent more time with her before the cancer returned—but she kept busy. Her sisters phoned or dropped by regularly, especially during the final months when Laura went in and out of the hospital, until the doctors said there was nothing left to do and she came home to die. I read an article about how positive thoughts create positive feelings. It broke down in laymen's terms how the brain works, all these electronic reactors, and how certain kinds of thoughts create certain types of reactions. I don't know what positive thoughts I can have. Freddy's sober, with a good job. Jan has a career, two kids and a husband. I never have to worry about money. That's positive. When I felt so well during the summer, it wasn't because I thought positive thoughts—but because I simply felt that way. But how could that be? It unsettled me to think I began feeling better after Laura died. Right now the birds don't sound the same as a few days ago. No pleasure in chores. How did I return so easily to this? Since the spring I've gone through the house from the attic to the basement, the garage, every room and closet, the kitchen—I own it. All the yard sales and sales on Craigslist to rid myself of a lifetime's worth of—shit, basically. Oh, there were a few items that were hard to let go like Laura's bike or Jan's saddle—but most of it—material things— televisions, stereos, a small refrigerator, odd furniture or Freddy's weights. Now I know the location of every single item in the house. It's windy and raining hard. I cancel my walk. Last night Jan called to say hello. I told her about Freddy staying here, and the opening, and how good Freddy seems to be doing. Jan suggested that I fly down on Thanksgiving. They usually spend holidays with her husband's family. I've only been there the one time I went with Laura. I wouldn't want to intrude. It won't be an intrusion there's room for one more. Had I thought about taking a trip—maybe to someplace warm like an island or a cruise? I could afford it and had the time. I told her I had, but really hadn't. I hated the very idea of cruises. Ten or twenty years back, hard to tell—Laura's family began taking an annual New Year's Eve cruise. No way I could be on a boat with Laura's family and hundreds of strangers for days where the high point of the voyage would be to celebrate the New Year drunk and forcing ourselves to be happy. Since the opening I wake in the morning and walk, or talk myself out of it. I have no appetite. I planned to paint the living room when the weather forced me indoors. Laura wanted to do it and would have. The ceiling's peeled and walls marked and scruffy. Last time she painted the room I watched her do it. Or caught glimpses as I slid in and out of the kitchen from my room for a snack or a Dr Pepper, eying curiously as she taped border areas, moved and covered the furniture, sanded scratchy surfaces, took a roller to the big spaces and a brush to the particulars. I don't want to go to Jan's for Thanksgiving. I hardly know her in-laws. I'd have to get a room. I'd have to rent a car because I wouldn't want to put anybody out. I'd have to fly. In Dunkin' Donuts I touch my moist fingertip to chocolate sprinkles on the napkin and place them on my tongue. I can hear them now, Laura's friends and family—me against the world or rather, the world against me. But it's not that. What am I supposed to do put on a happy face? You can't just loosen up and enjoy the bright side of life. It's not that simple. My father could paint a room second nature—cigarette hanging from his lips, can of cheap beer nearby, he worked full tilt, the way he did everything. One night during a deer season we got a snowstorm and he woke us early so we could track a big buck down. And chase one down he did. From six in the morning until four in the afternoon he tracked that buck. Finally, with only a few minutes shooting light left

54

he got a glimpse and shot that big animal in its tracks. He drove that deer relentlessly, all day, up and over hills and ridges, down steep slopes, over brooks and streams. It got worse after Ronnie died—his obsession with the big buck every year. He wouldn't settle for less. He entered the woods in the dark before sunup and didn't come out until dark—eating his sandwich on the move. Right up to when he died he and Junior never stopped hunting together. I surf the Internet looking for information on how to paint a room. Rollers and sandpaper I have. I'll need measurements to determine how much paint. I roll out the tape measure and make my way around the room, writing down the feet and inches, one wall to the next. Then I measure the ceiling and multiply the length times the width. Last night I dreamed of Ronnie. We were in the tree house and Ronnie brought his nudie magazines and our mother appeared and began to scold us then I notice her waving a dildo demanding we tell her where we got it. Ronnie looked so young like he did the last time I saw him and my mother looked old like the last time I saw her. And then Laura appeared and we were in a hospital room and she saw the dildo and I knew it was hers and started to say something but I woke up. I burp donut grease and flavored coffee.

/////

Home Depot had many brands of paint and color charts with dozens of variations, each color with its own name. They don't have paint ready to go it has to be mixed. I asked the paint clerk a lot of dumb questions and selected an expensive line and a color that closest resembled the one already in the living room. On the way home, I stopped at Subway for a turkey on whole wheat but got a meatball with melted cheese instead. I planned on going home working through the afternoon and eating the sandwich for supper. But I ate the sandwich soon as I'm home washed down with a Dr Pepper. Then I brought everything to the living room—paint, brushes, sandpaper, covering for the furniture, a ladder, rollers and masking tape. I've done nothing but walk around it all for days. I struggle over what to eat so I've been eating practically nothing but a few crackers—a piece of toast with butter. The few mornings I do walk I rush to get home and watch television. I like the reality shows where the theme is to embarrass someone about their problem and force them to change while the world watches. There are hoarders, drug addicts, gamblers. One guy became addicted to eating raw meat and other people live in filth. A skinny dominatrix of a woman hosts a show about fat people who can't stop eating. She documents everything the person eats during one week then duplicates it on a large table so the person and viewers can see all the chips and steaks and burgers and beers and pies and cookies and bacon sandwiches consumed in seven days. She verbally humiliates them until they cry. Then contestants lift bags of fat that weigh the amount they are overweight and she tells them that's what you are a bag of fat. The highlight is when she takes the contestant's stool samples and has them analyzed. Laura loved Halloween. She went all out and often made Freddy's and Jan's costumes. She carved pumpkins, put cutout witches and ghosts in front of the house, and made her own costume for when she handed out candy. Her family threw an annual Halloween party with a prize for the best costume. I put the bags of candy in the basket—Reese's Peanut Butter Cups, Almond Joys and my old favorite, Snickers. Helen says hello, haven't seen you lately. She caught me off guard. I've been busy doing lots of work at home. There's no one behind me in the line. I've gained weight. I ask is she doing anything for Halloween, pointing to the candy. No, she lives in a building—apartment. I spend the afternoon watching television or browsing through magazines. All of Laura's subscriptions still arrive regularly even though they've run out. There are health magazines, exercise magazines, magazines about herbs, magazines about nutritious foods. My body's changing—the weight returning with the overall lethargy. I've pain in the bottom of my back and can't get comfortable. I get lulled into an article about fats and what they do to the heart and arteries. Then read a recipe for a vegetable sauté with whole wheat pasta. I've gone over, given in. I've got chips and Dr Pepper and frozen dinners. My father kept beagles for rabbit hunting. They lived in the yard. There were usually two or three of them. My brothers and I had to clean the dog pen, and feed them. There was a female named Polly. One time my father bred her with one of the males. She had a litter and for some reason most of them died. It went on all night the puppies dying. My father called a vet to help but there was nothing to be done. I was seven or eight. He buried them in the back yard at the edge of the woods. I cried that night like I never cried before. My father threatened stop crying or he'd give me something to cry about. I remember walking to that spot at the edge of the woods and staring down over the remains. Once, I took a shovel to dig and find what had become of them. I dug several different spots but never found a trace—nary a bone. I consider turning off the lights and not answering the door but the weather's turned warm so I sit on the front steps with a bowl of assorted candy. There are so few children on the street now. On Halloween nights when Freddy and Jan were growing up the street swarmed with creatures of all sizes—for what seemed to be hours. Most of the families on the street had three or more kids. Now two children are rare, and some couples have no children at all. A few kids come and go—younger ones with their parents and within an hour, it's over. I put the bowl of candy on the kitchen counter, grab a Snickers and reach into the fridge for a Dr Pepper. The holidays are coming. I want to paint the living room as a kind of gift, or gesture to Laura. I'll start tomorrow. No, I won't set myself up that way—I'll wait until morning and see how I feel. Laura's sisters planned a memorial one month after she died, at an Italian restaurant—mostly Laura's extended family and friends. People were invited to say a few words, and many did, eloquently. I spoke briefly, mostly to thank everyone for coming and told them Laura would be happy to know. I sat in a far corner of the room, my back against the wall. A number of my in-laws approached and sat to converse with me. Laura's sisters gathered pictures from everyone in the family, and had them made into a movie—flashes of Laura's life—from infancy to the previous year's Fourth of July bash. There were even a few of me—a wedding shot—everyone voiced a spontaneous ah and looked over at me—a few from the early camping trips—one of Laura and me in a canoe on the pond. I can't recall ever being in a canoe with Laura. I couldn't wait for the event to end and wanted the entire post-Laura death thing to be over and done with—tired of people calling on the phone to see how I was doing, or to share their thoughts about how much they missed Laura. The hospice people visited to check on Laura and ask how things were going. Often one of her sisters stayed overnight. I didn't mind and felt as if I'd been transported to another world since Laura came home to die, that I lived in a separate time dimension with her in and out of consciousness twenty-four hours a day. I never slept more than a few hours straight. People came and went. Sometimes for a short time Laura gained enough strength to talk—she and her sisters reminisced about the past. Often, near the end, there were long silences. Laura mostly slept—a combination of being so weak and all the morphine. She woke fewer times, only able to nod a yes or no did she want more morphine? Each day passed like three. We rotated the care. I'd be alone, her older sister Karen would come in the morning and I'd try and rest. Then I'd take over later in the day and perhaps at some point Laura's younger sister Jenny would come. We mostly talked about Laura—how she'd been sleeping, how much pain she seemed to be in, when would the hospice person be there again.

/////

Laura's sister Jenny invited me to Thanksgiving dinner—
the entire extended family under one roof. Freddy has
to work Thanksgiving and suggested that I go to the
restaurant for the best turkey dinner I'll ever eat. Jan left
a message wondering if I had given any thought to flying
down for Christmas. I thanked Laura's sister—told her
maybe I'd take her up on the offer. I told Freddy if I felt
up to it I'd call when Thanksgiving got closer. But that's
the last thing I want to do, go to the restaurant on
Thanksgiving. My night out there sent me into this
tailspin. Each day I rise and it's the same. Do I want tea
and fruit, or coffee with cream and sugar and a Pop
Tart? Take a walk? Start the living room? It's hard to
beat Pop Tarts while propped up in bed. This morning I
chose to walk it might clear the head. I avoid the usual
route along the river road but walk back roads until I hit
Route 115 and turn around to come home. Everything's
gray. I have an idea—it's been years since I've been in
the woods and without much thought here I am driving

on Route 115 toward Bristol. You can still find a few farms and big wood lots out that way—including Bear Brook State Park. Sometimes on summer Sundays we went to the state park to picnic. My brothers and I swam and played all day. My father sat in a lounge chair sipped beer and smoked. He liked to peek at the girls and other moms. My mother applied sun tan lotion, fed us sandwiches, snacks, poured lemonade and warned us when our lips were too purple. What I remember to be a long drive is a half hour as I turn into the state park entrance and follow the road that leads past the pond where we picnicked. The pavilion and picnic tables are still there fifty years later though everything looks smaller, even the pond. Down the road, I turn into a parking lot where several hiking trails converge. There should be free maps but the container is empty. On a bulletin board under a plastic shield hangs a map of the park with an arrow pointed to a spot that reads YOU ARE HERE. One side there's Cross Park Trail, in the middle is Trapper's Loop and to the right, Three Hills Trail. I don't want to climb three hills nor walk across the park. Trapper's Loop circles around and returns back on itself to the parking lot. There are two other cars in the lot. One empty, and in the other a man sits with the engine running. I make my way across a narrow, slow running brook and up a slight incline to follow the trail marked by blue dots. Though warm for this time of year I wonder if my light jacket will be enough. By the looks of the scale on the map, the trail's no more than two miles long—an hour's walk tops. The trail winds through scented pine stands floored with packed pine needle beds then empties out into hardwood stands of straight tall trees mostly bare with an occasional dead leaf clinging. Wind blows crisp oak and maple leaves in circles. I follow the blue dots and the worn trail down along the edge of a marshy area where a large crane stands in absolute stillness at the edge of a small pond. I stop to watch. A few seconds pass silently until the bird seems to step into the air and with a great swoop of its broad wings, soars across the marsh and disappears over treetops. I remember a dream though I don't know if I had it last night or weeks ago. We're celebrating at one of Laura's sisters' houses. Laura's sisters are teasing me like they sometimes did when they drank a couple of glasses of wine. Oh loosen up they'd say it's Thanksgiving. My mother is here talking about the light and then Laura walks in and I tell her I'm tired of her sisters making fun of me. Laura's wearing a nightdress her skin looks remarkably smooth, radiating a pink-white hue. I wrap her in my arms. It's my mother but my arms go right through her and there's nothing there and everyone is gone. The trail leads up over a low granite knoll, and when I get to the top, I stop. To one side the late afternoon sun burns low in the sky. I never like the light this time of year. No matter what time of day it seems to blind me from somewhere on the horizon. On the top of an oversized granite rock I spy a blue dot and wind around and down a slow grade. All of a sudden, I get the feeling I'm being watched. I turn side to side and scan the area but see nothing. I move to step and hear a loud grunt. Looking to my right a large whitetail buck with its upper lip curled stands not more than ten feet away. I looked there a moment ago and didn't see him blending in with the brush but now his outline is clear and I fear he might attack—there are stories of bucks attacking humans, especially during rut. The animal lets out another grunt, then in one powerful leap and two bounds, with the late afternoon sun glistening on the tines of its marvelous rack—disappears. My chest pounds so hard I sit on a fallen log afraid I'll have a heart attack and die right here in the woods, my remains found by some deer hunter from Brewster. They'll have to get in touch with Freddy for identification. Who'll come to my memorial service? Who will assemble photos from my life and make the movie? I gather myself until my heart settles and look around to get my bearings but see no blue dots. I never liked watches. It was bad enough staring at the clock at work. Freddy urged me to get a cell phone. By the angle of the sun across the valley I make it to be around four o'clock. This means an hour of daylight left. I tell myself not to panic and try to retrace my steps but circle the wrong way and get disoriented. It will be a long cold night in the woods. I have no food nor did I bring water. Because of the way the trail loops around, I'm fairly certain that if I walk in a straight direction I'll intersect it. Using the top of the ridge across the valley as a fixed point, I walk down the hill. Junior taught me how to get around the woods with or without a compass. He said if you think you're lost in the woods, first thing to do is settle down, stay calm, and find bearings. Once while deer hunting my father spent the night in the woods. He tracked a deer late into the afternoon, finally took a shot, but only wounded the animal. By the time darkness had settled he'd gone too far to make it out safely so he simply hunkered down for the night with a flask of whiskey and can of sardines, emergency supplies he always carried. I wish I'd brought a candy bar. At the bottom of the hill I have to cross a brook. Because of my low elevation, I can no longer see the opposite ridgeline but I have to climb in order to stay in a straight line. Crossing the swift, but low-running brook I slip off a rock and my right foot goes under into the icy water soaking through my walking shoe. I charge up the hill, running as hard as I can. I must get out before dark. I'm crashing through tangles without looking when a branch snaps back into my right eye. The pain stops me in my tracks. I can't open the eye. There's a reality show I watch about people who shouldn't be alive but they survived some horrific ordeal—people lost in the desert or woods or at sea. I imagine falling, breaking a leg—helpless on the ground without food and water, cold and wet for days, weeks, fending off bears and coyotes. I've done significant damage to my eye but it will have to wait. The pain is overwhelming but not so bad as my will to get out of the woods. I squeeze it shut, press my right hand over it and continue swiping branches away with my left hand until the opposite ridgeline comes into view and I'm sure I'm walking in a straight line. I stumble over stumps and rocks, thinking about Laura—in the kitchen making her beloved chili—leaping in the air, her fist raised when she pitched the winning softball game in her family's annual Guys vs. Gals—the first time we made love how I had trouble and Laura said maybe she can help and she did what she did, and it helped—her particular glow when she headed for work at the shoe store—her corpselike body in the living room—the morphine drip. Could she have opened her eyes during that instant? I hear a car slowing down in the distance, straight ahead. Then the engine stops and a car door opens and closes, and then again an open and closed door. My eye tearing profusely I press on. Every time the pain begins to surge I press hard as I can with my hand. Faster and faster I race, brushing branches aside with newfound fervor, trying to keep in the direction of the slamming car doors. I pay no attention to the growing discomfort in my eye—I have to get out of the woods now. The sun has set and the woods darkening. I think of shouting but don't want to waste my shortened breath. In a stand of young pines, I hear a car engine ignite. It sounds directly in front of me but I can't see through the thick short pines. My body trembles momentarily. Lunging ahead, I run as fast as I can, straight for the sound of the idling car engine. Hand over wounded eye I place my left arm in front of my face for protection and barrel through the last branches into the open and with a resounding thud fall directly onto the hood of a car. The man in the driver seat's face widens in shock. Then the second man's head pops up from his lap.

/////

I had an abrasion on the surface of my eye. It hurt enough that I knew I'd better go to the emergency room and they made me wear a pressure patch and use antibiotic ointment. It was plenty sore at first, and swollen. Lying in bed watching television with my good eye I binged on pizza and soda. Freddy called every day to check in did I need anything? At the follow-up appointment they removed the patch and everything seemed fine. In the dream I'm running through the woods being chased by a giant bird swooping down and pecking at me with an oversized beak. Every time the creature attacks it lets out a caw-like shriek. I try to hide in thicker cover but get tangled unable to move while the bird circles overhead. I free myself and once in the open the bird is relentless in its quest. I read somewhere about turning to face your demons in order to put an end to their pursuits, so I stop in the middle of a small meadow and watch the bird dive. I take off my jacket, swinging it wildly over my head, shouting come and get me as the bird drops down and attempts to pounce. I whack it full-force with the jacket and knock it to the ground then pick up a large rock with both hands and smash its head until the creature is dead. At the edge of the woods I see two animals copulating—deer, of sorts. They're not animals but humans—Laura and another woman. The woman is on all fours and Laura penetrating her from behind. I turn and run in the opposite direction, straight into a small pond where I'm trying to swim but Laura is dragging me under. I wake in a sweat. It's Thanksgiving morning. Against my objections, Freddy insisted on dropping by tonight. The restaurant's open for special holiday hours and closes at six. Around eight he arrives with a bag full of delicacies and a half bottle of wine. The wine is for me. Freddy drinks sparkling water and serves fish chowder, green salad, turkey with his own sausage-sage stuffing, cranberry sauce and a duck breast with some kind of glaze—all of it unlike anything I've ever eaten. Not the same as cranberry sauce out of the can Freddy remarks, what we grew up eating. Laura had always been a good cook, her dishes were simple and side dishes, like cranberry sauce were never made from scratch. During dinner Freddy talks about his job, his daughter who he's seeing again, and a woman he met in the program. They're taking it slow. She's been sober for eleven years. He hasn't been around so doesn't know how long the paint supplies have been sitting in the living room. The accident set me back I tell him, I planned on finishing the job by Thanksgiving. The wine lightens my head after a few sips. He asks do I remember the Thanksgiving when Laura dropped the cooked turkey and it smashed on the floor and she picked it all up, removed the meat from the bones and ordered us to remain silent when her family arrived to eat. I've forgotten. Laura told her family that she decided to debone the turkey before dinner that year. What they didn't know wouldn't hurt them. We laugh. Freddy pours me another glass of wine then serves apple crisp with his homemade ginger ice cream. We reminisce about other holidays and he confesses about the Christmas he found his electric trains hidden in the garage and set them up on the garage floor when Laura and I were out. Then he gets serious and asks do I miss Laura? I'm nearly through the second glass of wine and slurring a bit. I do miss her—think about her every day. Suddenly I feel an urge to tell Freddy about that night, how I knew that she'd had enough—she'd all but told me so. How I waited until her sister left and Laura fell back into a deep sleep. I want to tell you something. It's about your mother. I open my mouth to speak, but the wrong words blurt out. She had a dildo. No sooner do I utter those words I realize my blunder. He looks at me confused. I fall silent for a moment then apologize. That's not what I meant to say and for the life of me I don't understand why I said it. It's a little more information than I need to know he says. Oh Freddy, it's the wine I say. Freddy asks what do I want to say and I try again. Freddy—when she was sick—near the end. But I stop. I apologize again. He tried to make this a real holiday for us and I let him down. I haven't let him down Freddy says. It's natural for me to feel distraught—after all, this is the first holiday in over thirty years that I haven't been with Laura. Anyone would be out of sorts. He reaches over and puts his arm on my shoulder. It's okay Dad. It's okay. I begin to cry uncontrollably and Freddy remains by my side until the tears subside and then we clean the dishes and make small talk. This morning I'm resolved to change my ways. I felt so good during the summer, doing chores, walking, eating well—and I let it all slip away. I feel like I have cold coming and make a cup of green tea. In the freezer I find a loaf of whole wheat bread and defrost two slices for toast. After breakfast I go through the food cabinets and freezer to throw away the Pop Tarts, Sugar Pops, Fig Newtons, chips, coffee and various frozen dinners. A sinking feeling overcomes me when I recall last night. I think I have a hangover. How could I say such a thing to Freddy? On the other hand—what if I told him the other truth? The temperature hovers at freezing. I put on my shoes and coat, then for the first time in many weeks take a walk. By the time I reach the river road I'm out of breath and my leg muscles tightening. It will be a while before I'm back in shape. In town I drink a cup of herb tea at the café. Eve says nice to see you it's been a while. I tell her there's been a lot going on lately. At home I find an ambulance in front of the Coviello house. Mrs. Coviello's outside and her husband with an oxygen mask lying on a stretcher being lifted into the back of the ambulance. Once the attendants have him inside, she steps in and the ambulance races off down the street, siren and lights blazing. Several neighbors mill about, talking amongst themselves. Sounds like Mr. Coviello suffered a heart attack. Fifty, fifty-five one woman says. Another one adds that she just talked with him the other day he looked fit as a fiddle. I stand there among virtual strangers, although I've been their neighbor for who knows how long? Back home I find all the paint supplies in the living room. Today I'll begin. My first task is to mask things off which I do, occasionally stopping to look out the window and see the crowd of onlookers dwindle until finally nobody remains. Laura knew all about the Coviellos, and their children. She probably mentioned them to me on numerous occasions, but I couldn't recall anything except Mrs. Coviello's first name Vivian and her husband Robert. I can't remember having a conversation of any length with either of them. I finish masking and begin to sand the walls with various gauges of sandpaper as instructed by my online research. By mid-afternoon I'm hungry but I've thrown most of the food out so I walk to the market and buy some salad greens, brown rice, green tea, tofu and tuna fish. I've been buying the junk food at a convenience store and now when I approach the checkout registers I look for Helen. She smiles says no see you for a while and I explain I haven't been feeling well. I place the groceries in my backpack and on my way home, it begins to snow lightly, first snow of the season. Thoughts of Mr. Coviello, dinner with Freddy last night, and my fiasco walking in the woods swirl like the flakes around me. I can't forget the astonished looks of the two men in the car—I imagine Mrs. Coviello sitting in the hospital waiting word from a doctor—the image of Laura mounting a woman from behind in the dream—telling Freddy about the dildo—I see myself on the living room floor, suffering a heart attack with no one home to phone an ambulance. Snow begins to mix with rain. When I arrive home, the Coviello house is quiet. I fix a

71

salad and a cup of tea then wipe down the table, wash the dishes and return to sanding the living room ceiling and walls. Early in the evening, I hear a car pull up next door. I recognize the Coviello's daughter getting out with Mrs. Coviello who looks shaken, taking her daughter by the arm and being escorted into the house.

/////

Breakfast is wheat toast and tea. Then I paint the living room ceiling. Lighter furniture I move into the dining room. The sofa and big chairs are covered with plastic throw cloths. I fill the paint pan fasten it to the ladder then climb cautiously, roller in hand. When I finish one small section I refill the paint pan and move to another. First coat covers smoothly. Waiting for it to dry I fix a cup of mint tea. Two days eating right and walking already I feel better. Cars pull up next door. I peek out the window to see friends and relatives. I think I recognize the children. He must have died. Yesterday walking the river road a pickup truck approached me from the opposite direction and I thought nothing of it until it drew closer and made to pass. It was Junior. Without a second thought, I waved. For a brief moment, Junior let his foot off the gas and gave a quick toot of the horn as I turned to watch the truck disappear down the road. The back of his truck was strewn with bumper stickers: SUPPORT OUR TROOPS, GOD BLESS AMERICA and MCCAIN/PALIN. I hadn't seen Junior since Laura's funeral. I didn't vote in the last election, though Laura was excited about Obama. I haven't voted in years. I don't understand politics and nothing really changes no matter who's in office—they're different sides of the same coin. I wonder what Junior might be doing driving through town. The hunting season just started, maybe he's been out in the woods. He still works on the police force despite eligibility for retirement—and he always takes vacation days during the annual deer season. He might have been heading to or from one of his deer stands. When I try to recall exactly when and why Junior and I lost touch I can't. I went to college, and Junior thought me a coward, and always believed that I inadvertently caused Ronnie's death. I remember his wedding. When his firstborn Judy got married, I went to her wedding but by the time Junior's second and third were married I wouldn't go. Laura argued that my differences with Junior were no reason to take it out on my nieces and nephews and she went to the events alone. Later Junior declined the invitation to Jan's wedding after Laura insisted that he get an invite to my disapproval. Throughout the morning more cars park in front of the Coviello home. I saw one of the neighbors walk to the door with a casserole dish. I paint the second coat on the ceiling then fix a tuna sandwich on whole wheat bread. I still miss the fat, salt and sugar but in a few more days my system will be used to the better food. I read how you become addicted to certain things—not only drugs and alcohol but also food and lifestyles—healthy or otherwise. You can get addicted to feeling good or feeling bad. All those years, decades really, I felt

74

what I felt. Judging others never was my style so why be judged? Laura said it was depression. She didn't say it really, but I know she thought it. And it's what her friends and family told her. Laura once said that after the kids were grown maybe we should go our own ways but by the time both the children were out of the house Laura had settled into her routines—she loved tending the house, spending time with friends and family, she lived as if I weren't there. She lost hope that someday I'd turn anything around. At the market I buy the newspaper and find Mr. Coviello in the obituary section. Robert Coviello, fifty-eight, left behind three children, seven grandchildren, his wife a brother and two sisters. He died suddenly. People come and go next door, but each day fewer and fewer until it seems things are back to normal. This morning I heard a car door slam and looked out to see Mrs. Coviello back her car out of the driveway and leave. That's it. Somebody dies, there's the initial shock whether you expect it or not—then the days that follow, dream-like, and then one morning you wake you're still alive life must go on and you go out—to the store, or maybe to visit a friend, or back to work. When Ronnie died, it set me back months—every morning a wave of dread washed over me. At first, I overheard my parents talking about how they didn't know what they were supposed to do. At night Ronnie appeared in my dreams saying that he had not died and there he'd be just as I remembered him, walking and talking. Then I would wake to the slow realization that Ronnie was gone and would never again be here. Laura told me that Mrs. Coviello had a part-time job. Maybe she's already going back to work. When Laura died I moped around the house for weeks—I had no appetite, no motivation. Then slowly I found my way into the regular routines. I feared someone would confront me about what I did, maybe one of Laura's sisters or one of the people from the hospice. Now it feels fixed in the past, my secret. I'm not the first person to do such a thing. When I finish painting the walls and trim, I bring the leftover supplies to the storage room. Once again I sit in my recliner and page through magazines that continue to arrive in the mail, along with bills for them that I don't pay. I watch a little television—cooking shows, self-help shows and the news. Mornings I rise and walk, afternoons to the market, find assorted chores to do around the house, and evenings I rest. I'm feeling better again. Last night six inches of snow fell, the first storm of the year. I shovel the driveway and front walk. When alive, Laura often came out to help. I always told her not to it was my only regular chore. It's light snow, easy to clear and I pile it neatly each side of the driveway. I walk next door to the Coviello home and shovel the driveway and walk. Mrs. Coviello opens the front door to thank me. I needn't have she could use the exercise and an excuse to get out of the house. No bother I say, and sorry about what happened to your husband.

/////

Another foot of snow fell, the heavy, wet kind. I strain to
clear the driveway and walks. A man in a truck plows
the Coviello's driveway. She hired him for the season. I
wonder how much he charges. Back inside the house
the heat won't turn on so I take a look at the furnace and
click the emergency switch. I wave a flashlight over
things as if I know something then flick the thermostat
again. Nothing. The heating company has a backlog and
won't get anyone out until the afternoon. By the time
the repairman arrives the house is fifty-five degrees. I sit
in the recliner wrapped in a blanket watching the
news—the weather people predict a snowy winter. The
furnace needs a part and he says he'll return later and
finish the job. It's about six years old, the furnace. I
remember when the old furnace once went out in the
middle of a blistery cold night in February. Laura, the
kids and I used electric heaters and boiled water on the
stove for two days. We sat in the living room, the four of
us under blankets, talking to each other more in those

two days than we had in months, drinking coffee and hot chocolate eating peanut butter and jelly sandwiches. Who knew then that some day when Freddy's divorce was finalized he'd get drunk and crash his car into a tree? Or that I'd be here alone, wrapped in a blanket, everyone gone one place or another? I'm craving a meat-eaters pizza though I planned vegetable stir-fry and brown rice but I don't feel like cooking in the cold. I order a pepperoni, sausage and meatball pizza. The repairman returns and in a few minutes, I hear the furnace ignite. I offer him a slice but he declines, doctor's orders he says, putting his hands over his rotund belly. Within an hour, the house warms and it's like it never happened. I remain in the recliner, eating pizza slice by slice, watching reruns of *Have Gun—Will Travel* and *Wagon Train* on the Western cable station. Outside, the wind tears through trees, gutters and window shutters. I go to bed early, but have trouble sleeping—tossing about in bed, thinking about Mr. Coviello, several years younger than me, lying in a box in the frozen ground. It comes any time. Healthy or not—look at Laura. I sit up, turn the television on, channel-surf, stop for a few minutes here and there settle on *Patton* with George C. Scott, the part of the story where the general has to publicly apologize for striking a shell-shocked soldier. Ronnie and I saw the movie together. We rode our bikes to town. That old theater's boarded up now but I hear they're going to reopen it and put on plays and concerts. When we got home we delighted my father by singing the praises of Patton one of his heroes. My stomach gurgles. The pizza hasn't settled. I fall into a light sleep, wake, fall asleep and wake again. Near dawn, I dream of

Laura, she's wearing a long furry coat and talking about the snow. She says she's not dead. I tell her about that night, about what I did, and how I watched the ambulance take her away and later at the cemetery they put her in the ground. But you didn't do it, she says. You turned the key in the brake. I wake, calling Laura's name. Daylight creeps in around the blinds. I turned the key in the brake. What did she mean? I put the kettle on for tea, toast two slices of bread but I have no appetite. I burp pizza. I wish I had a Pop Tart. I talk myself out of walking then change my mind, put on my coat, hat, boots, gloves and strike out for the river road. My lower back aches, maybe from all the shoveling. What about the key and the brake? I stay close to the side of the roads where plows have piled snow high. At the river road, sidewalks are clear near businesses and homes but along the uninhabited stretches, I have to walk out into the breakdown lane. Cars pass, at times too close for comfort, and at one point a plow truck swerves to avoid me and the driver beeps the horn. A moment later, a sander passes whipping out a mixture of salt sand, also maneuvering around me and beeping the horn. I haven't thought about how the snow could interfere with my walks and the usual route won't be safe. Not halfway to town, I cross the river road, turn around and walk cautiously home. In some ways, I'm relieved. If the snow keeps coming, I'll have an excuse not to walk. I sit back in the recliner trying to masturbate thinking of Mrs. Coviello. I shovel her driveway and she invites me in for coffee and one thing leads to another. Nothing's happening. I read about diet and exercise and maintaining a healthy sex life into your senior years. I go to the bedroom for the computer, then, sit at the kitchen table looking at a site that has different categories and decide on Big Boobs to see massive growths that look unnatural on young women with skinny bodies. I click the Teens category and began to get hard looking at various young girls posing, or in the process of having hardcore sex—but I feel a tinge of guilt at looking at girls young enough to be my granddaughter so I switch to the Mature category where I look at women who could be in their thirties and some decades older. One woman reminds me of Mrs. Coviello—the same coloring, age and shape posing in different stages of undress. I stop there, imagining it to be Mrs. Coviello. Things simply aren't working. I feel empty and cheap, shut the computer and open the kitchen blinds. A veil of sadness shades the sunlight. My neck hurts I think I'm coming down with a sinus infection. Jan phoned and pressed me about taking a trip to Chicago for Christmas. I hesitated, making flimsy excuses why it wasn't a good time but Jan persisted. I had nothing to do. I needed some activity outside the house. I needed to see my grandchildren and they needed to see me. She would handle all the flight arrangements, pick me up at the airport and make it as easy as possible. I didn't know what to say so I caved in. Jan wanted me to go for a week. She said it would be best if I left a few days before Christmas, that way I could avoid the travel crunch. Would Jan's husband's parents be in town? Yes, but I'd have the guest room they'd stay at a nearby hotel. When I suggested I stay at a hotel and her in-laws take the guest room, she said not this time, it had already been arranged and her in-laws insisted. I only met Phillip's parents once, snobs and conservatives—not that I care much about the nature of a person's politics. I dread having to leave home, leave the state, fly, stay over at Jan and Phillip's house and spend time with Phillip's parents. At the same time, I feel a tinge of guilt. What kind of man doesn't want to see his grandchildren? I don't really know mine. I'm committed to the trip and will suffer through it—unless of course I get a serious flu, or have an accident or an emergency root canal. On the news I saw how flying's become a nuisance with long lines, body scans, major delays and crammed flights— especially around the holidays. For the longest time after Ronnie died his things remained in the bedroom. He and I shared a dresser. There were two small drawers on top, Ronnie's stuff on the right mine on the left for socks and underwear. Of the four full-sized drawers, I had the upper two and Ronnie the lower. In the closet, every day I had to face Ronnie's coats, boots, shoes, his baseball uniform and cleats. His baseball glove sat with a ball in it on his bunk the way he left it the night that he died. On the wall hung pictures of his heroes Roger Maris and Mickey Mantle, and strewn about the room were his copies of *Sports Illustrated*, *Field & Stream* and *Outdoor Life*. At one point, I gathered all of the magazines and piled them in a corner. I wondered when my mother would clear everything out, if she ever would, but she seemed so distant and withdrawn I hardly thought it fit to ask. Besides, she had all she could do to deal with my father's increased drinking, his shouting, calling her names and the occasional slap or punch. I spent more and more time in my room, avoiding everything, watching television hours on end—game shows, situation comedies, Ed Sullivan on Sunday nights—Sunday was my worst night of the week since it meant school the next day. I never liked school but after Ronnie died I especially couldn't stand the idea of facing other kids. Sometimes I played sick to get to stay home from school—especially on Monday mornings. Mother would take my temperature, tell me I'm fine, and send me off to catch the bus. I discovered one technique that worked: I'd wake up during the night, go to the bathroom and force my fingers down my throat in order to throw up. It got so bad she took me to the doctor for what seemed to be some kind of stomach problem. The doctor said, right in front of me, the problem is probably not in his stomach but in his head. Eventually my mother simply went along and let me stay home whenever I said I didn't feel good. With more snow forecasted for the overnight, I drive to the market for groceries. Snowy roads will prevent further walks. There'll be no more debates should I or shouldn't I? I'll get exercise shoveling. There'll be plenty of snow. I pass through the natural food section ignore produce altogether and in frozen foods stock up on dinners and Pop Tarts then press on for a case of Dr Pepper, pretzels and chips. I know there must be a bit of truth to all I've read in Laura's magazines and books. But it's all too much for me right now. During the summer and fall I did feel better—but something all the while pressed and probed, trying to sneak through cracks in my defenses. What does it matter anyway? How long do I have left? It's my right to make myself comfortable. After all, there's no guarantee that all the exercise and healthy eating will do anything when your number's up.

/////

Jan made my travel arrangements. Freddy is driving me to the airport. On my return I'll take an airport shuttle to Brewster where Freddy will pick me up. I've been mooning around the house, eating, watching television and trying to convince myself I have a cold or flu, perhaps walking pneumonia—maybe a sore throat, headache, body pains. Jan phones. My grandchildren can't wait to see me, nor can she. Only a miracle will help—a slip on ice, broken limb, a minor heart attack or stroke. I pack my clothes, and gifts from the mall—toys for the kids, a scarf for Jan and tie for Phillip. I never had a knack for buying gifts. A big snowstorm swept through two days ago, knocking out the East Coast, shutting down airports everywhere. If only the storm hit on the day of my flight. Within twenty-four hours, things were back on track. This morning the weather is clear and when I go online to check the departure it's on time. Freddy arrives with coffee for the road and loads my bags into the car. Am I ready? Ready as can be. The drive to the Boston will take an hour and a half. Freddy came early allowing for traffic delays and long lines at check-in. Turns out to be no traffic. We'll make good time he says and talks about the restaurant and the new woman he's been dating. When I return he wants to bring her over for a visit. He confesses that he had a slip-up—two weeks ago, on a night off, at his apartment alone he never saw it coming. In the middle of watching a movie, he got up, put on his coat, walked down to a bar and had four drinks. He still doesn't know why. It's not like he'd been feeling bad but just upped and went to a bar, as if some unknown force directed him. The drinks hit him hard since it's been so long. After the fourth, he went home to sleep it off. It can happen he says. It never goes away, no matter how long. The next morning he went to a meeting first thing. He thinks it's a good idea my going to Jan's for Christmas. It's my first Christmas since Laura died. Last Christmas, she was under hospice care. Her sisters dropped by with food, talking about past Christmases, sharing anecdotes about Laura. Freddy does most of the talking. AA meetings. His daughter. Opening his own restaurant some day. I've been planning to tell Freddy about the last night with Laura. This will be a good time—the two of us out on the road. But I start and stop, each time unable to find the words. The ride seems unusually quick for such a long distance. As we get closer the airport, I'm afraid that I missed the chance. Freddy is instructing me about checking in, and what to expect. At Logan International he misses the turnoff to the gate and must circle the airport road. This will take several minutes as he loops around the airport exit then turns back in to the entrance. I fidget in the seat, sip on the last of the cold coffee I've been nursing the entire ride. As the car approaches Gate A, I tell him there's something I want to say. Something I've been holding in, about Laura, in the end, when she was in hospice. The only thing that kept her going was morphine. We pass Gate B. She was tough and never complained, from the beginning right up to the end when she'd ask for more morphine. So there had to be a lot of pain. The sign for Gate C appears. That last night when we were alone—I'd entertained the idea before—but I thought it only a matter of days. And who was I to make such a decision? Gate D. She opened her eyes and looked at me for a moment, as if trying to say something but she didn't. I wish that she said something—anything that might have brought it to some kind of, resolution. But she didn't. She opened her eyes for a few seconds, and then she closed them. As we approach Gate E, Freddy says he knows what I am trying to say—that under the circumstances he might do the same thing. My hands are trembling as we pull up to the front of the gate. But who are we to play God? Freddy says, he didn't think I believed in God. That I had the opportunity to be there in the end—I should take comfort in that. We sit in Freddy's car for a few moments. Outside, people rush in and out of cars and taxis, pulling bags from trunks. Freddy places his hand on my shoulder. It's okay, Dad, you did what you thought you should do. You weren't the first. I ask can he forgive me? Nothing to forgive, he answers. We exit the car. He opens the trunk, removes my bag and carries it over to the curb. Have a great trip he says, and give my love to Jan and the kids. I'll see you next week in Brewster then he motions to hug me and we embrace. He hands me my carry-on and points towards the door. Inside I take my place in the long, winding line. Telling someone would help, I thought. But at the moment it hasn't. If God really exists, why did someone like Laura have to suffer? I wonder what Freddy really thinks. The line moves slowly. Babies and toddlers hang on their parents. The older, restless kids run around until their parents call them back. Behind me a woman of seventy or more smiles every time I turn, as if expecting conversation. Ask me where to? Where from? I won't get trapped. I have no grandchildren photos if she should break hers out. After registering, I move to another line where I empty my pockets, remove my shoes and go through a pat down. Once through the gate, I've an hour before boarding, and walk around looking at various eateries and stores, deciding on a cinnamon bun and cup of coffee. The bun is sweet and sticky. I lick icing off my fingers. Jan got me a window seat. Beside me in the middle sits an oversized Asian boy, fifteen or sixteen wearing a fluorescent green t-shirt and his fleshy arms hang over the armrests. His iPod, I learned that from Freddy, is so loud each beat shoots right through me. He sings along, off key. The old woman who stood in line behind me is in the aisle seat, absorbed in a paperback book. Mostly I stare out the window, down at the earth below through scattered clouds—focusing on roads and varying landscapes—eyeing insect-like cars on thin-strip highways, trying to measure the scale of it all, imagining someone on their way to work, or to visit family, or to a chemotherapy appointment being driven by a loved one. Who knows what Christmas has in store? I think back on my childhood, there is no single Christmas I can remember, but flashcube glimpses from some collective memory bank—my mother's ham dinners and the family sitting around the table, the anticipation on Christmas Eve with my brothers trying to get to sleep, my father drinking too many beers passing out on the sofa, a photograph of me and my brothers wearing pajamas sitting in front of the tree on Christmas morning—Ronnie holding a Monopoly game, I'm holding a box containing an electric train set, and Junior holding a single shot .410 gauge shotgun which would be handed down brother to brother. Laura decorated the inside and outside of the house, played Christmas music the days leading up to the holiday and sang along, her favorite song "Little Drummer Boy." She baked Christmas cookies and breads—I always loved the orange-cranberry bread with the lemon-butter icing.

/////

I forgot how much Jan reminds me of Laura. Not only her physical appearance but in the timbre of her voice or the way she raises her left hand, index finger pointed upward when emphasizing a point. They live in a suburb, neat houses and well-kept yards outside of Chicago. Jan says that neighborhood people are friendly and host gatherings at each other's houses on weekends. Her children, Abby eleven and Eric fourteen, have many friends on the street but now that Eric's taken up sports he's off on his own. Seems there's always a practice or a game. Like her mother, Jan decorates her house, plays Christmas music and sings along. She works as a college administrator but took the week off to spend time with me and get ready for holidays. With two days together before the kids' vacation and her in-laws' arrival, we run errands to the supermarket, the mall for last-minute gifts, the package store—Phillip's parents love their martinis. Jan shows me around the area—Abby's dance school, the baseball field where Eric plays, the college where she works, the best Italian restaurant around. We lunch at a place famous for its burgers. Jan talks a lot about Laura—how much she misses her and still has a hard time believing she's gone. Her voice cracks and at lunch she cries and I eat nearly an entire jumbo burger and fries. I haven't spent any time around children in decades. Eric is aloof prone to one-word answers. Abby calls me Grandpa and smiles when answering my inquiries about school or her dancing or the cat, Mr. Candy. I hate cats. I dislike the idea of pets in general though when the kids were growing up Laura insisted that we get a dog. When the in-laws arrive the household changes from subdued to hyperactive with several conversations going on at once—between Laura and her mother-in-law or Phillip and his father. I find it easy to blend into the background. Phillip's father John's my age. He still works, in finance and goes to a gym to keep fit. Not getting any younger, he says, slapping his hands on his flat stomach. Phillip's mother Ruth seems younger, but something about her face doesn't add up. She has no wrinkles, when she smiles nothing moves— her skin looks stretched out. They dress well, and name-drop the stores where they shop though I don't know one from another. Ruth flashes her jewelry, fond of stretching her hand out and studying her diamond. John prides himself in wearing a jacket and tie to dinner. I haven't brought a tie. John talks incessantly about money and politics, bending Phillip's ear, offering advice on investments and going on about how the Democrats will socialize the country and bankrupt everybody. Phillip listens intently, nodding his head in agreement, occasionally chiming in with a short comment of his own to which John replies, you bet, and then continues his diatribe. Occasionally, John corners me and I tell him that I don't follow most of that stuff but John pays me no mind. You mark my words he tells me, everything we've worked for, everything we've stood for, this president is going to dismantle if we don't get him out in the next election—and Mitt could be the man to do it. I hated Mitt Romney when he was the governor. It wasn't that I care that much about politics—all my years working for the state had opened my eyes to the corruption in both parties. But when Romney was governor his cuts had been particularly harsh and unfair. He came off as another slick rich guy. I don't tell John this—even when John says Mitt did a great job turning your state around. I count down the days to my departure. At night, I go to bed as early as I can get away with—watching television in the guest room. John insists that we say grace at the dinner table. Jan had warned me ahead of time. She considers herself an agnostic, though she sometimes goes along with Phillip when he takes the kids to church. She says maybe it's good that the children have something to believe in. I resent John's sanctimonious tone, when he bows his head and thanks the Lord. I stare off into space and refuse to say Amen when he finishes. After Ronnie died I stopped believing in God though I doubted it before that. Laura sometimes referred to a higher power of sorts. She didn't attend church regularly and said if there is something up there, what matters is who you are not that you go to church. Christmas morning, John and Ruth arrive early, wearing their holiday best to watch the children open gifts. The kids tear through wrappings, briefly stopping to inspect the contents then move on to the next. Toys have changed. Now it's electronic games with funny names. They don't look like toys. John and Ruth bought Abby an elaborate dollhouse that dwarfs the doll that I gave her. I didn't bring a gift for John and Ruth but they presented me with one—a tie. I gave Jan the bottle of perfume the saleswoman helped me select and to Phillip the striped tie the most expensive the department store offered. Phillip and Jan give me a sweater and Ruth asks is it cashmere and Phillip answers yes. The gift opening ends in a matter of fifteen minutes then we sit down to an elaborate breakfast of pancakes and bacon. John asks am I coming when they go off to the church. I answer no and John looks at Jan who looks at Phillip who looks at his mother who looks at me who turns and walks upstairs to the bathroom to shave and shower. I have the place to myself for nearly two hours while the others are at church. I can't wait until I am back home. The day drags on. We sit around the dinner table long after we finish eating, and the children grow restless. Abby leaves to play under the tree with her gifts and Eric disappears to his room. I become overheated in the new sweater that I decided to wear. John's talking about the country's eroding moral fiber, the problem of immigrants bleeding the system, Obama and his fellow socialists giving the country away while raising taxes. He offers non-stop advice to Phillip and Jan about what they should be doing with their money and how they should be preparing for their children's college education. All the time Phillip nods his head in agreement and I begin to see him as a mini-version of John. Ruth keeps her wine glass full, maintains a smile, and occasionally chats asides to Jan who remains mostly quiet. An hour or so after dessert the women rise from the table to clean after dinner. I do the same despite their objections—I need to move around after all the food I tell them but I really want to get away from John. Phillip and John retire to the living room and I hear John's pompous voice from out there. Ruth touches my arm, a little too intimately for my comfort. Do you miss her she asks? I stiffen when she fails to remove her hand. Yes, I do miss her and back away grabbing a pan to dry. You and Laura were together a long time she says. Thank goodness they flew home this morning. Jan's not one to say bad things about folks but I can tell her feelings towards them are lukewarm. I fly out tomorrow but yesterday when Freddy phoned to say Merry Christmas he warned that a Nor'easter had been predicted. I spend most of the day watching the weather. In the evening Freddy phones and says a foot of snow is predicted in Boston. In all likelihood, the flight will be cancelled and as it turns out it is. The busiest travel time of the year has been derailed by a mighty storm. I panic at the thought of extra days here but I'm helpless to do anything about it. Phillip takes us to lunch. I'm quiet, thinking about getting home, settling into the recliner, watching television and indulging in my favorite snacks. I order a burger and fries. Phillip says he heard I became a vegetarian good to see me back on the flesh. He'd rather die a few years earlier than not have steak, as he bites into a piece of sirloin. Abby asks Daddy, are you going to die? Jan answers that we all die some time but Phillip was just kidding around with Grandpa and he wasn't going to die any time soon. Grandma Chase died Abby says. I know she did Jan says, and she's in heaven now. Phillip looks at Jan and Jan back at him. Why would an all-loving God give humans cancer? I don't ask. In the morning, I hear Phillip leave for work and go downstairs to breakfast with Jan. She got me a flight tomorrow. The kids slept in. Abby appears later and sits up on my lap while Jan makes her pancakes. Jan looks at us, and smiles. Abby asks will I come visit again? I tell her I will. Jan makes another stack of pancakes for Eric and covers them on top of the stove. Jan and Abby go to the market. I watch television in the living room. Eric slept until noon and when he comes down he passes the living room without so much as a good morning. I watch the weather station to catch the New England forecast. Tomorrow will be clear. In the morning I wake anxious and melancholy. During the night, I dreamed of Ronnie. We were ice-skating at night on the beaver pond behind our house. A full moon shone down like a stage light. Suddenly, at the opposite end of the pond Ronnie crashed through the ice. The water in the pond was never deep enough to be over our heads, but Ronnie began flailing around, calling for me to help him. I skated towards him and the ice under my skates gave way as I moved but somehow, I kept afloat remaining one skate-stroke ahead of the breaking ice. Ronnie's calls became more frantic. Despite making progress across the pond I couldn't get any closer to Ronnie. By the time that I reached him he'd gone through, the ice sealed up—everything solid. I shouted Ronnie's name, skating around the end of the pond, stopping and banging the end of my stick on the ice. The light of the moon illuminated the water below. No sign of Ronnie. The pond had sucked him up. Our ride to the airport is mostly quiet. Jan looks tired after all the entertaining. I insist that she drop me off at the gate and not park and wait with me. I lean over and kiss Abby. Jan wraps her arms around me, kisses me on the cheek and thanks me for coming. The flight home feels twice as long as the flight down. This time I have an aisle seat. Images from the previous week flash through my mind—of Abby and Eric, Jan and Phillip, Ruth and John. I never had the chance to tell Jan about Laura. Maybe I never made the chance. I wanted to tell Jan I was sorry. Sorry for never being there when she was growing up. Sorry for never being there, for Laura. Sorry for never being there, for Freddy. When the plane touches down I feel as if an ordeal has ended. I never expected to see home again. I breathe easier. Freddy and his new girlfriend are waiting when I get off the shuttle van in Brewster.

/////

Nearly two feet of snow fell in the storm. I call someone
to plow the driveway. Trying to shovel the walk I'm
easily out of breath, and forced to stop every few
minutes. When the man finishes the driveway I drive to
the market thinking about what Freddy said—every day
you can change—you are able tell yourself you won't do
something anymore—you have a choice. I turn the
options over. Good food means possible long-term
relief. Bad food brings short-term relief. Freddy
suggested that I join a gym and get a personal trainer. I
have the time and money. In the produce department
greens, reds, yellows and oranges—apples, bananas,
grapefruits, green vegetables, peppers, cauliflower and
fresh herbs. Get plenty of color in your diet they say. I
pass through produce to frozen foods and stock up on
dinners, then grab potato chips on sale two for one, a
case of Dr Pepper and several boxes of Pop Tarts. No
see you for a while Helen says ringing me up. I've been
away. Family. At home silence covers the house. The

smell of fresh paint lingers. I sit in the recliner watching television. When I'm hungry I fix a frozen dinner or fill a bowl with chips. I used to fantasize about a day when the kids were out of the house and Laura and I would live separately. I could find a little place of my own, free to do as I please without the feeling that I'm being judged. I miss her comings and goings, the various activities, phone conversations with friends and family when I'd keep an ear out to hear what she said. One of the cable channels runs a reality show about hoarders, right through the afternoon. I watch one episode after another. A lot of them are men, and for some the hoarding didn't come on until middle age. Women hoarders seem more willing to make change—they want to be able to have a guest over—they cry when confronted with their problems. The men are stubborn, and resist, they get angry. Snowstorms have pounded the area for two weeks. I hire a specialist to come out and remove snow from the roof. There's too much up there and it could cause damage. Driving's sloppy and difficult. Snow's piled high both sides of the roads. On better days, I go to the market to stock up on groceries, and hunker down in the living room. Snowdrifts reach the roof. I've gained back all the weight I lost over the summer—and then some. When I shovel, I have to pace myself so I don't end up with a heart attack on the walk. I don't know what to do with my time. How much of it do I have left? Six months? A year? Ten? What might have happened had Laura not got sick? I think of Ronnie. He looks the way he looked when I last saw him—a teenager. I think about my promotion to office manager. The days are long. I stare at the digital clock for one hour straight trying not to miss any minute changes but my attention wanders, and I lose track at nine or ten minutes into it. After Ronnie died my mother began going into states of disassociation. My father, or Junior or I might be talking to her and she'd be staring off into space. She might be looking at you but instead looked through you and didn't hear a word. Doing dishes or ironing clothes she'd suddenly stop and gaze at something only she could see—like she was someplace else. Her bouts came and went, but continued right into old age when I'd visit her and suddenly she'd drift away. She had night terrors and woke up screaming at my father who'd try and calm her down. I could hear them from my room. Freddy phones to say he would drop by with a pizza. One glance at me and the inside of the house he can see things have turned around. I haven't picked a thing up since I got back from Jan's. My shirt and pants are stained, my face unshaven. We eat pizza in the living room. Freddy asks how am I doing? I'm doing fine. He suggests that I might want to get out of the house it might do me some good. Then he asks me what am I going to do? When? Now, this year, the next few years. I can't be sure maybe I'm doing it I say. You can't just stay home and do nothing. If that's what I want to do then that's what I might do. Besides, I've never been one to do much of anything. Why change now? He's worried. I'm fine. He says there's lots of things that I can do like volunteer at a local hospital or the museum in Brewster. I might even want to find some part-time work. Big snowstorms meant that my father was out on a truck, plowing, twenty-four, thirty-six or more hours straight. I cherished those times. The house was tension-free and my mother more relaxed. She made frozen dinners and we ate on trays in the living room watching television. Ronnie and I took our sleds to nearby Fox Hill, wearing ourselves out until dark. My father eventually arrived home tired and irritable with a case of beer over his shoulder. He ate a meal and drank until he passed out or grew belligerent and ended up arguing with my mother. Ronnie, Junior and I were in charge of shoveling the driveway and walks, and dread to us if the job did not meet my father's expectations. In the summer we cut the grass and in the fall we raked leaves and in winter shoveled. My stomach drops whenever I see a plow truck. It reminds me of him. Sometimes during a storm my mother would meet him out on the road. She'd bring food and a thermos full of coffee. I can see him in the truck sitting at the steering wheel—a small man with receding hairline, a day or two's worth of stubble on his face, cigarette dangling from his lips. In bed I listen to the wind. Judging by the frequency of the furnace turning on and off, the temperature must be sub-zero. The house shakes with each wind gust. I fall to light sleep and wake. Thirsty, I walk out to the kitchen for a glass of water. Back in bed I'm restless trying to get back to sleep. The phone rings around six and I wonder who's calling so early. I let it ring—they can leave a message. Days have been running into each other. It takes a few moments before I determine this to be Thursday. When I worked, I dreamed about retirement days when I could sleep in every morning and not be forced out of bed by the alarm. But now I wake every morning by six or seven wide awake. I put coffee on and place two Pop Tarts in the toaster. On the phone message, Junior's wife Tammy asks can I call her? Something must have happened to Junior. There'd be no other reason for her to phone. My Pop Tarts pop up. I pour a cup of coffee with cream and sugar then sit down at the table to eat. My hand shakes when I raise a Pop Tart to my mouth. After breakfast, I phone her. Junior suffered a stroke. He's in intensive care at the medical center in Brewster. He lost movement in part of his body and can't speak. They don't know to what extent he might recover. Tammy says she thought I would want to know. I thank her for the call and ask how you holding up? Best she can under the circumstances. I tell her I'll go to the hospital later in the day and maybe see her there. She says don't feel any pressure she just thought she should let me know. Junior was his father's son. He looked like him, drank like him, smoked like him and owned his temperament. Before securing me the state job, my father connected Junior to the police academy when he came home from the service. I try to think back to the last time I talked with Junior besides the few brief words at Laura's wake and funeral. Junior treated Tammy the same way my father treated my mother—condescending tones of voice—off-handed derogatory remarks. I never witnessed anything but always suspected that Junior hit Tammy. It was the rumor. At the hospital Tammy and her oldest daughter sit besides Junior's bed. Junior's hooked up to various machines and appears to be sleeping. Tammy thanks me for coming and I ask how is he? No change. Junior came home from work last night and said he didn't feel well. He picked at his supper then went in the living room to lie down and watch television. Tammy cleaned the dishes and when she went out to the living room, she found Junior on the floor and called the ambulance. Had she not been home, he could have died. Tammy looks older than I remember. Her hair's white, her face wrinkled from years of smoking. First time Junior brought her home they were in high school, my parents were having a cookout in the yard and I sat at the other end of the picnic table and watched as she ate a hot dog delicately, her brown hair up in a beehive wearing a short yellow cotton dress while she answered my mother's questions about her parents, and school, and did she know certain people my mother knew. He finally got to sleep Tammy says. He needs rest right now. I stand there in an awkward silence. There are no other seats and my niece offers me hers but I insist that she keep it. Junior is pale, the top of his head bald with gray strands around the sides disheveled. I stay as long as I think is long enough then say my goodbyes and tell Tammy if she needs anything to call. I'll be back again tomorrow. Light snow falls on the drive home. Ten to twelve inches are predicted. One time my father took me to watch Junior play hockey. Junior, always the aggressor, got into a fight with another boy. The two had been going after each other with hard checking since the opening of the game. My father shouted out to Junior not to take any of that kid's shit and just clobber him. The next time the boy checked Junior, Junior dropped his gloves and slugged the boy. My father began to yell at Junior to knock his teeth out. Junior beat the boy up and was thrown out of the game. My father got into an argument with the referee insisting that the boy had it coming. He'd already downed the better part of the half pint of whiskey he kept in his coat. The boy Junior whipped stood on the other side of the rink being tended to by his coach—his face bloodied. The coaches and referee threw my father out of the rink and he stormed out hollering that they hadn't heard the last of him. The snow keeps on coming right through the night. The snowiest January on record—the white stuff piled so high that at a local mall parking lot snow removal trucks have made a snow mountain already one hundred feet high. The media has dubbed it Mount Mall and claim that at the rate we're going it won't melt until July. Late in the afternoon, the man comes to plow me out. Snow along the walkway is heaped to my shoulders on each side. I can barely throw the snow over. Tammy phoned and left a message when I was shoveling. Junior's condition has stabilized and they're hoping to move him to a rehabilitation center tomorrow. I microwave a fried chicken dinner and sit down with a Dr Pepper to watch evening news that focuses on the day's storm, and an elementary student who brought a syringe to school and pricked several students. I don't want to get into a routine of having to visit Junior. Why should I? During Laura's illness, I never saw him though Tammy visited once or twice. It's funny how the women stayed together that way. Laura and Tammy and they weren't really related. I watch *Family Feud* and eat potato chips.

/////

I eat Chips Ahoy at the kitchen table thinking of the day Junior took Ronnie and me fishing at a remote pond in Belchertown. We rode our bikes to a trailhead, and hiked two miles uphill where someone had left an old flat-bottom rowboat and one oar. The boat only seated two so Ronnie and I took turns in the boat with Junior while the other fished from shore. It was the first time I saw Junior smoke a cigarette. He threatened Ronnie and me don't say a word to our father. We'd heard rumors of big, native brook trout and fished for hours without a bite. My mother packed us lunch but we forgot water, and on several occasions quenched our thirsts from the clear, cool pond. The sun beat hard that hot day. Junior said the water would be ok to drink because the pond was spring fed. Towards the end of the afternoon Junior and I were in the boat and heard Ronnie scream from shore. Junior paddled us over and we found Ronnie holding up a two-and-a-half-pound brook trout—the biggest any of us had ever seen outside of a picture. My mother fried the trout and served it with baked beans. Later, we began throwing up and shitting uncontrollably. It took twenty-four hours for the water parasite to work its way through our systems. Suzy and I are driving on the old Brewster Road where at night you come over the last of the Brewster hills and see the city lit below. Suddenly the dark sky above the city turns red then orange the air begins to vibrate and Suzy asks what's going on? All the lights in the city go out and the car loses power. Rolling down the hill I have no headlights and can't apply the power brakes or steering. Two jets swoop down from behind us low and cacophonous they descend on the city as the car steers uncontrollably off the road, rolling over several times before coming to a stop in a gully. I can't remember the first time I dreamt that dream—but I know it's a serial dream and by the time the car goes off the road I always tell myself this is a dream. I wonder where Suzy is now. What happened to her in life, did she settle down, have kids, is she one of those old hippie grandmothers eating vegetarian and wearing Birkenstock sandals and long skirts? Maybe she became a banker, a lot of those hippie kids did. Junior watches me enter the room. There's nobody else here and I hadn't planned on being alone with him. He lost use of his right side and his right eye and lips are distorted. He can't talk. As I sit in a chair near the bed he follows me with his left eye. I ask how you doing? Junior grunts. We stare at each other in a protracted silence. My stomach gurgles. Heartburn from last night's fried chicken dinner and potato chips. This morning I stopped at Dunkin' Donuts for two honey-dipped and coffee. I search for words but nothing.

Junior grunts, seems to be asking for something. Water. You want some water? He grunts again. I fill the cup and bring it to Junior's lips. Junior sips and water dribbles down his chin. I wipe it with a napkin. I hope that Tammy or one of the kids shows up, to break the silence—to relieve the tension. Lots of snow this winter I say. Junior fixes on me with his left eye. I make occasional facial expressions. After what seems a half an hour but is only fifteen minutes I clear my throat and tell him I have to go. Get better. I'll come back tomorrow. As I turn to leave, Junior grunts one more time, longer and more urgently than before. He extends his left hand. I step towards him and put my left hand in his. He squeezes hard for someone in his condition, and looks at me with the one good eye and grunts the longest one yet. Then he lets go of my hand and I leave without another word. Junior will have to retire now. I can't imagine him recovering enough to return to the force. What might it be like to love your work the way Junior loves his? Though we were out of touch, over the years I read in the newspapers when his name appeared for some noble action in the line of duty. He even delivered a baby in his cruiser. Several times he won citations. He also had a reputation for being a tough guy and once or twice there were investigations for things like roughing up a teenager or other excessive force. I never knew action or glory—only boredom—day after day, week after week, shuffling papers, watching the clock, the endless small talk—the release in the pit of my stomach at five P.M. and the return of the knot at the alarm the following morning. At least Junior found something he liked and got to do it. What could it have meant, his squeezing my hand that way and grunting? I hear animals from our bedroom and look out the window to see a group of cats, frantically digging at the grave where my father buried the dead beagle pups. I race to the yard where they're tearing and clawing at one of the beagle pups. Every direction the pup turns, one of the cats heads it off. The beagle has several bleeding wounds and finally the cats get the pup down moving in for the kill. A shovel leans against the basement bulkhead. I grab it and return to the frenzy, swinging wildly at the cats, catching one smack on top of the head its brains splattering in every direction. I swing the shovel wildly at the other cats until they run off. The pup is on its side, bloody and crying a high-pitched sound that reminds me of a wounded rabbit. I scoop the pup in my arms and run to the house where my father meets me at the door angry and ordering me to return the pup to its grave and bury it. I tried to explain that the pup is not dead we must get it to a vet. Put the pup back in the ground he says or he'll hit me over the head with the bloody end of the shovel. I wake to the ringing at four-thirty in the morning. Junior's dead. I know before picking up the phone to hear Tammy say that he threw another clot in his sleep. I offer condolences. Does she need anything? Nothing at this time—she'll get back to me when she has more information. Because Junior's a police officer, there'll be special arrangements. She'll have to sort things out. I hang up the phone, brew coffee and sit in the silence of the living room as morning comes to light. I think of death—how it comes like a storm then passes without a trace. Afterwards, you see a fresh pile of snow, the ground is wet from rain, the sun shines and birds sing and cars pass by and jets fly high. All those years Laura and I went through the marriage in our own separate worlds—coming and going, exchanging information about the kids, jobs and things to be done—the years we slept in separate rooms. Gone. Now Junior is gone. Forty years my only living brother lived one town over and I can't remember more than a half dozen times we crossed paths. I have to call Freddy and Jan later in the morning but for now I remain in the recliner. A new batch of Laura's magazines arrived. Older ones are strewn around the house. I pick up the most recent *Vegetarian Eating*, and page through, stopping indiscriminately to look at perfect photographs of shiny vegetables—spinach, lettuces, kale and broccoli, oranges and carrots, purple eggplants, red apples and radishes, yellow squash and bananas. It's mostly advertising. My frozen chicken dinners consist of mashed potatoes, fried chicken and corn. But there are dozens of other ingredients on the box, mostly chemicals and additives. Everyone from my youth is dead. I close the magazine and toss it on the coffee table. Years passed with no real intimacy between us. Decades slipped past and no contact with Junior. I can't remember my father's funeral. Like Junior he went in his sleep. When my mother died, Junior and Tammy had people back at their house and I didn't go, much to Laura's disapproval. Death is personal, I said, everyone has a right to deal with it in his own way. My mother died slowly, in a nursing home, shrinking away to a ninety-pound skeleton. I phone Jan and Freddy. Freddy says we should go to the service together. He'll pick me up. I like Freddy now. And I like him being around. I wish Laura were here to see him—how he turned out okay after all—responsible, sober, making a name for himself as an upcoming chef. Over the years, I watched Laura's worrying take a toll on her. It seemed things were always going wrong with Freddy. Sometimes she'd simply break down and cry, she felt so helpless to do anything. When she got sick, her sisters told her she had to worry about herself now—there was nothing to be done about her son. Freddy lived away during much of that time, although there were occasional phone calls for money that Laura would send. Junior's family and friends will be gathering at Junior and Tammy's place. I'll be a hypocrite if I go.

/////

The suit I bought for Laura's funeral fit tightly—I had to leave the jacket unbuttoned. At the wake, being the brother, I stood in the reception line, next to Tammy and her kids greeting hundreds of people most of whom I'd never met. I didn't want to do it. Freddy said I really should it was the right thing. People offered condolences, sharing personal stories about Junior, what a great man my brother had been. Your brother was a cop's cop one officer said. So many people it felt like it wouldn't end. This morning at the funeral service I half-tune in as various policemen, the minister and Junior's grandchildren speak. Two police motorcycles escort a line of cars, so long it takes nearly an hour to get everyone parked at the cemetery. An American flag drapes the casket, and there's a twenty-one-gun salute followed by a portable recorder that plays "Taps." Freddy says that we should go back to Tammy and Junior's place, just for a short time, I'll be glad we did. I agree on the condition that when I give Freddy a signal, we'll leave. I sit in a living room chair while an occasional relative I hardly know approaches with small talk. Nearby Freddy converses with Junior's kids, how much the area has changed, and their pasts, and how time flies. Freddy brings me a plate of food—a ham and cheese sandwich, salad and chips. I eat half the sandwich and nibble on the chips. After we've been here about an hour I give Freddy the signal. The hardest part is saying goodbye to Tammy. Something tells me this might be the last time I see her. She makes me promise that I won't be a stranger. The ride home is quiet. Light snow falls, enough that Freddy has to turn on the wipers. Too bad about Junior he says. I look out the window at the snowy landscape, clusters of houses, strip malls and the last patches of woods standing. They're gone now—my mother, my father James, Ronnie, Laura and Junior. During the baseball season my father, mother, Ronnie and I piled into the station wagon and drove to watch games. Junior invariably hit in the winning run, or pulled off a key play at shortstop. My father shouted out instructions from the stands. Watch that second base runner he's going on the pitch. He's pitching high to the outside tap one into right field. My mother didn't like the cold rinks in winter but Ronnie and I tagged along to Junior's hockey games where Junior had a habit of throwing questionable hits on the opponents, and scoring winning goals with seconds left in the game. The girls loved Junior. He always had a girlfriend and stole Tammy from Jimmy Wilder, the high school quarterback. If anyone should go to college, it should be Junior my father said. Junior could play baseball or hockey for any team. But it was not to be. Despite his sports prowess, Junior never made an effort at school and rather than try for a sports scholarship he opted to sign up for the military. The doorbell rings, I slide the blind to look out. Mrs. Coviello holding a dish in her hands. I open the door and she offers her condolences about Junior, and spaghetti and meatballs in case I should get hungry. I thank her and invite her in. No, but she was thinking of me knowing that it must be a tough time. I insist, just a few minutes, and she takes me up on it. I haven't done housework in weeks and have to clear mail, clothes and magazines so she can sit on the sofa. Sorry, I haven't been keeping up with the housework lately. No worry. Besides, she adds, housework is overrated. I smile and offer coffee or tea but she declines. How have you been getting along? There are good days and bad days she says, it's hard to be alone. I study her closely, she's a beautiful woman—dark wavy hair, shining olive skin, a few extra pounds but carries them well, buxom and curvy, legs crossed in her jeans, brown leather boots, her tight woolen sweater. She excuses herself, her daughter's coming over. I help her with her coat. If I get hungry heat the dish of spaghetti in a microwave. I thank her as she disappears down the snow-banked walkway. Who can masturbate at a time like this? The thought of Mrs. Coviello in black pumps, stockings and a teddy can't bring me around. But I try. It's funny about sex how the idea of it never gets old even if you do. There were years, however, in the past when I hardly gave it a thought. I imagine the two of us lost on a Saturday night in loneliness and abandon, taking a momentary hop-skip-and-jump-of-recklessness—a few cocktails, the kind of talk that lovers somewhere must talk, a dildo. Doesn't everyone deserve at least one secret pleasure? Those two in the state park parking lot—they had theirs. Two men meeting out in a remote woods. Perhaps they were married and had families. Or maybe one of them. Sweet mysteries of life. The room is littered with papers, cans, magazines, books, dirty clothes and dishes. I read that our gene blueprint can be made to change for our destinies, through lifestyles that are fun, enjoyable and energizing. Maybe it's an ad. I microwave the meatballs and spaghetti and open a cold Dr Pepper then turn on *The Biggest Loser*, a show that follows people around for months as they exercise and diet to see which one can lose the most weight. Months earlier I was lighter, eating differently, occupied with chores and walking. I slept better and felt better than maybe ever. Or did I simply tell myself I felt so good to account for the effort it took, every day, in the face of Pop Tarts and fried chicken, walks or the television? I haven't connected with anyone. Not even to see Eve at the café in town. Every morning it's the same thing—coffee or green tea—chips or fruit—meat or no meat—Dr Pepper or no Dr Pepper? Too many decisions and tests every step of the way. It just keeps snowing day after day. I hunker down in the recliner, trips to the kitchen for food, the occasional bathroom run. Now I pay the guy who plows to clean the walk with his snow blower. I only go out for groceries, buying a week's worth of everything I need. Some nights I fall asleep in front of the television. Jan phoned. Told her everything was fine I can't wait for the better weather when I can go outside to the yard and garden. Freddy phoned and we promised to spend an afternoon together and include

Freddy's daughter. Tammy phoned just to say hello and tell me how much she missed Junior. Next week is the first anniversary of Laura's death.

/////

I've been dreaming of Ronnie. In one it's some futuristic landscape, a world where the very few have what they need, and have-nots swarm in hordes around the edges, raiding malls, stores and houses. Ronnie and I scrounge for our lives, wear rags and steal scraps of food. It rains. Slow steady rain. We look for some place dry where we can rest. A mass of people huddles on a hill. Let's go there I tell him we can sit and take some comfort. In another dream an unseen force pursues us inside a building from room to room. We hear and feel this ominous presence—but can't see it. Finally, the force begins to let out roaring moans. I wrap my arms around Ronnie and decide I will attempt to scare the thing off. That I can make terrifying sounds too and we begin to roar back and forth. I watched Laura's sisters and the nurses do it. Then they showed me how in case she should need more. It didn't seem to take much to do the job. She didn't deserve to suffer—all that mess inside of her—the pain never went away. It snowed that night, five or six inches of the light fluffy stuff. All the biking and hiking, special foods and drinks—she never stood a chance against nature. Laura had always been active, eaten well, had a good attitude. She was a great person. Can't think of anyone better. It wasn't Laura I rejected, but being with her demanded something from me that I didn't have. Going to one family cookout meant going to all family cookouts—all family holiday celebrations, all vacations and birthday and anniversary parties—all the christenings and New Year's cruises. There would never be another free weekend. She said she didn't ask for much, but needed a little loving, even if only once in a while. I just couldn't. You can't or you won't she asked? I never seemed to be able to get close to anyone, even if I wanted. I wasn't the type to take her out for dinner, or have a romantic evening at home. I type in "Senior Volunteer Brewster, MA area" and pages pop up—an industry—one site after another—senior legal services, senior dating services, senior health services, senior money management services, services to help seniors find ways to volunteer, senior Christian services, senior Jewish Services, the Massachusetts Senior Center Directory, The Gay and Lesbian Senior Citizens Alliance, The Retired Seniors Programs of Brewster with its monthly calendar of events like Nature Art Exhibit, Native Art Exhibition, picnic at the Breezy Picnic Grounds Waterslides, Poster Making Contest, Friends Book Sale. Volunteers are needed in the public schools, local museums, nursing homes and hospitals. The last time I went to Dunkin' Donuts, they had a display with applications and a sign said they were hiring. I've noticed all kinds of people working there.

Hispanics, an Indian immigrant, a woman who wears one of those things on her head—an older man around my age, high school kids. Perhaps working a few days per week might be what I need. I can donate the earnings to a charity of my choice rather than do volunteer work. I got a flyer in the mail and went on a whim. Brand new condominiums in Harmony, bordering a conservation area loaded with hiking trails, a pool. I could sell the house and come out with money to spare. I made an appointment with a woman name Maria, who I'd imagined to be exotic with her mysterious accent. She turned out to be from Ireland, thin, pale skin, gray hair, she smelled of cigarette smoke. There were studios, one-, two- and three-bedroom units all slight variations of each other with shiny new kitchens, lots of chrome and granite, bedrooms with their own bathrooms, big windows and balconies with views overlooking the woods. It was five minutes from the interstate but you'd never know it—that's what Maria said. I tried to imagine life there. I could get rid of everything in the house— everything Laura and I shared. I could start anew. Eat right. Walk in the conservation area. Call one of the online senior dating services. Swim in the pool. Volunteer or work part-time. There wouldn't be enough hours in the day. It was a lot to think about, I told Maria. I'd need a little time. They're going to go fast, she warned. At the Dunkin' Donuts they were out of applications but the manager said I can fill one out online. I got coffee, a honey-dipped and a chocolate sprinkle. Perhaps Laura was a member of that secret tryst club—those people for whom life seemed only worth living when done in secret. Was it one of those lustful kinds of affairs? Or the rendezvous more like real life—regular talk, of kids, daily activity, friends, husbands and wives? Maybe a glass of cheap wine or a can of beer—sometimes, maybe they didn't have sex at all but hugged and kissed and that was good. I know that men pay women at the local motels. Elsewhere is where you find what's not here—if only for a fleeting afternoon—a Saturday night that you wait for all week. Henry's wife eventually moved the family, Henry followed. I don't think Laura expected that. It hurt her deeply. After Henry left she become despondent, took months for her to become her old self. While it was no long-term affair, and had never been officially consummated, I took pleasure in Margaret's arms. She promised she could make me very happy. I had a hard time with happy. A year ago there wasn't any snow on the ground. Nothing looks the same now. I drive up and down the little roads, made narrower by all the snow. At last, I find her row. If I leave the car, there's no room for another to pass but I leave it anyway. I don't remember how far down the row. Snow's over two feet deep, frozen at top, a crust that gives way with each step down to my upper thigh. Five or six steps I'm out of breath. Each time I break through I have to pull myself out. Most of the gravestones are buried. I'll never find Laura in this winter wasteland. I stop and look around. A tractor-trailer runs through gears out on Route 115. It's been quite a year. I have no idea which grave belongs to her and struggle hand over foot through a snow pile—I wipe snow away from the front of a stone believing fate will have it and this be Laura's place of rest. Then I try another then another but to no avail. I keep up my efforts until I am fully out of breath, practically unable to move in the waist deep snow. I stand for an undetermined length of time until finally breathing solidly again, I follow my footsteps back to the car. Seized by the urge for a hot drink I decide to drive to the café. It isn't until I park my car, get out and walk to the storefront that I notice the sign in the window—COMING SOON: THE RISING SUN BAKERY. The café is closed. The sun glares on the window and I shield my eyes to have a look inside. Someone might be in there and I could find out what happened and maybe learn Eve's whereabouts. The space is empty, not even a chair. They cleaned the place out one night I hear a voice, and turn to see an older man standing behind me. They owed back rent and other bills the stranger continues. Came with a truck in the middle of the night and took everything with them. Any day you can change Freddy says, you can simply say no—I'm not going to do that today. I sit down in front of the television with a frozen dinner and Dr Pepper, click the remote but the television won't come on. I bang the remote nothing happens. I could turn the television on manually but don't. What a cold place to be, out there on those rows, Laura, Junior, James and Elsie, Ronnie. I take a swallow of Dr Pepper and glance at the piles of books, magazines, dirty plates and glasses, empty chip bags and Dr Pepper cans, the sticky surfaces, empty pizza boxes, overstuffed and smelly trash bin, unpacked suitcase from the trip to Jan's two months previous, furniture tossed with odd shirts, pants, socks and occasional underwear, broken television. I wish I had some kind of reference point. What does it take to face this mess? I sit minutes, maybe longer. My frozen dinner is getting cold. Suddenly I step up from the recliner, find my coat, hat and gloves and walk through the front door down the walk out into the street. The frozen, plow-caked snow makes crunchy sounds under my boots. The sun shines. A white sea shimmers in the frigid air. My breath shoots in fixed measures as I stride down the street. Here and there chickadees flit atop snowbound hedges. At the end of the street I pause at the river road look down one way then the other. It's bare. Plows and sanders have done their job. The breakdown lanes, where I usually walk, remain snowed-in making the road tight for two cars passing in opposite directions. Walking safely will be difficult. I look to the left and right again. I see a yellow-lined asphalt road, snow banked to the tops of telephone poles on either side and above it all a winter blue sky.

quale [kwa-lay]. *Eng.* n 1. A property (such as hardness) considered apart from things that have that property. 2. A property that is experienced as distinct from any source it may have in a physical object. *Ital.* pron.a. 1. Which, what. 2. Who. 3. Some. 4. As, just as.